VIRGILLIA

VIRGILLIA

GILDA CIANI SFERRA

VANTAGE PRESS
New York / Los Angeles / Chicago

In memory of my beloved daughter Adrianne Gaetana Sferra, whose love was like a torch, brightening every life she touched.

May her soul rest in God's everlasting light.

The Madonna Della Civita whom the Vina family venerate in Virgillia appeared on Mount Civita in Itri, Italy, from which the Vinas migrated at the turn of the century. The Madonna first appeared to a mute shepherd who then found his voice. The villagers built a sanctuary in her honor. People came to this sanctuary from all over Europe to worship her. She has wrought many miracles throughout the centuries.

Other immigrants from Itri, Italy settled in Cranford, Rhode Island. They built a church in her honor in Knightsville where every July 21, the day she appeared in Itri, centuries past, they feast in her honor.

ONE

Virgillia was in love. She knew she was in love from the moment David Long had entered the architectural firm of White and White, Inc., and had enclosed himself in the executive, glass-paneled office that was plainly visible to Virgillia and the ninety-nine girls in the stenographic department.

Right now, lying on the lumpy mattress, wedged between her four sisters in the stuffy bedroom of the Vina flat, Virgillia momentarily forgot her surroundings as she thought of Donald Long.

It must be close to seven o'clock and time to get up, thought Virgillia, for she heard mama opening and closing the door of the icebox. Maria prepared her soups for the large family early, because she said the vegetables would be more nourishing sliced and boiling in the large soup pot with whatever reasonably priced meat the butcher saved for her, than they would wilting in the icebox. Virgillia respected her mother's wisdom, but right now she wished she would make less noise so she would not be disturbed in plotting how to reach Donald Long.

The early morning light coming from the parlor window through the large window that had been built in the wall separating the parlor from the bedroom etched the huge, green trousseau trunk at the foot of the bed. Ma kept her best linens in it. The green curtain gathered on a pole across one side of the room improvised a closet for the Vina clothing, while the shelf above it stored summer or winter clothes, a

1

whisk broom, shoe polish, hats of all shapes and sizes, plus most of the odds and ends that had to be placed out of the children's reach.

On the left side of the room stood a battered dresser with a chipped statue of Saint Theresa hugging a spray of roses. Before Virgillia fell in love she often lay awake wondering if papa would some day replace the green curtain with rolling doors as some of the apartments were being remodeled in the neighborhood, but with so many youths to feed, papa would never have enough money to buy rolling doors.

The industrial growth brought about by the First World War, which took people out of poverty during 1918, did nothing for the Vinas because the family kept increasing. This morning, however, Virgillia was not thinking of rolling doors and green curtains, she was billowing on fantasy. Ben Worth who worked with Donald often brought Donald's closely written notes to the stenographic department. The girls were reluctant to type the tedious reports because, they said, Mr. Long was a perfectionist and he could detect an erasure, no matter how well it was done. Ben had turned to Virgillia for help. Secretly, Virgillia was thrilled to do Donald's reports. She lived in the hopes of one day presenting the finished work to him. Donald Long had been in the firm two weeks, but as yet she had not had the pleasure of making contact with him because Ben, who liked to quip with the girls in the stenographic department, used Donald's work as an excuse to make his many appearances during the day, taking Virgillia's finished reports as soon as she completed them.

Her sister Tommy, who slept beside Virgillia, stealthily moved off the bed and tiptoed to the parlor. Virgillia sat up and called in a loud whisper, "Tommy, take off my negligee!"

Tommy ignored Virgillia as she clumsily slipped herself into the whispy, flimsy gown.

"Tommy, you ripped it!" yelled Virgillia.

"Jumpin' elephants, Virgilla. I thought you were asleep.

I've been wanting to try this dainty lacey negligee since you bought it."

The whining plea in Tomasina's voice was lost on the irate Virgillia, who whisked the coverlet off the bed and dashed into the parlor after Tommy. Around and around the center table they ran, Tommy hugging the negligee.

"Virgillia! Tomasina!" sternly called their father from the kitchen where he was busily pouring cereal into bowls for his brood. For a moment Tomasina and Virgillia paused in the escape and pursuit, then Tommy dashed to the kitchen, dodging her father's tail, thin figure, tripping over the pot in which mama was shelling peas.

"Oofa," Maria raised two chubby palms impatiently. "In the name of the Father, the Son, and the Holy Spirit." Maria crossed herself to ward off the evil spirits who would upset her day. She was a round, comfortable sort of woman who felt marriage meant having children and accepted with resignation the seven girls who had come to bless her marriage with Francesco.

Francesco was right, thought Maria. Virgillia was their most difficult daughter. What was the rumpus now? Francesco caught Virgillia's shoulder as she dashed after Tommy and gently shook her.

"Virgillia, your two older sisters, Rosalia and Luisa, never acted as you are doing, at your age. At twenty they were responsible married women."

Virgillia shook herself free. The comparison of the virtues of her two older sisters versus her own was a tender subject between Virgillia and her father.

"I don't care what Rosalia and Luisa did at my age, papa. I want my negligee. I saved lunch money to buy it, and I don't want Tommy playing dress up in it."

Rosalia and Luisa used to get up at five o'clock, as ma does. They used to dress quietly, prepare breakfasts, make beds, wash breakfast dishes, and then leave for their work at the factory. "Good qualities desired by good husbands," continued Francesco, hoping to awaken mature responsibility in preparation for Virgillia's eventual marriage.

"Yes," agreed Maria. "Papa is right, Virgillia. Don't you see how well married Rosalia and Luisa are today?"

"Oh, gooey," said Virgillia. "They were matched by two odd men. Rosalia's husband, Guiseppe, is a milk toast. Rosalia had to open a shoe shine parlor for him. Now she must manage the store and their home. Giuseppe has no sense of responsibility."

"Maria, we almost sank on that old ship *Columbus* coming to America. Were we saved to have a disrespectful daughter like Virgillia?" Francesco stood straight and tall staring at his daughter with bewildered green-blue eyes.

"No, Francesco, we were saved to bring good mothers into the world. Virgillia will mature like Rosalia and Luisa after she marries," soothed Maria.

"I'm not being disrespectful, pa. I am only stating my opinion." Virgillia did not want to give her father cause for concern, but she had to make him understand that she was a person in her own right and not a carbon copy of Rosalia and Luisa. Besides, she thought hopelessly, his ideas were archaic, stemming from the Old World from which he and Maria migrated. She was living in the United States of America in the early twenties. Papa and mama had never made the transition of accepting New World ideas. Definitely there was a generation gap. Virgillia could only be herself, just as mama and papa were themselves.

"I am an individual, papa, and must express myself in my own way. Only then can I feel like a person; don't you understand, papa?"

Francesco shook his head negatively.

"No!" he said emphatically.

"Francesco, don't waste good time on Virgillia's strange

4

ideas. We have come to a strange land, the language is different, the foods are different, the climate is different, the thinking is different, and Virgillia is picking up all the strange ideas.
Perhaps we should have sent her to work at fourteen the way
we did with Rosalia and Luisa instead of allowing her to go to
high school. But don't worry, Francesco, as soon as we find her
a husband she'll be as good a wife as our other daughters."
Maria spoke confidently, trying to calm the inward qualms
about Virgillia's strange ways.

"You are right, Maria. It is our purpose to straighten her
way of thinking with a good Italian-American husband," agreed
Francesco.

Tommy, glad that pa's attention had centered on Virgillia,
carefully folded the negligee and placed it over a kitchen chair,
then dutifully ate her cereal, careful not to smack her lips as she
usually did, she wanted to escape pa's further censure this
morning.

"Tommy, stop taking Virgillia's things. You're much too
young to be wearing Virgillia's clothes. Pick up every pea you
spilled!" Pa infused a stern note in his voice, which Tommy in-
stinctively knew meant she should obey.

Francesco heaved a sigh and shifted his weight from one
foot to the other. He wished he could shift as easily the weight
of Virgillia's strange ideas, the daughter he least understood.

Born in a small village on the snow-capped Italian mountains, near Rome, Francesco and Maria brought the understanding of their culture to America. Francesco sensed the
wonderful freedom of thought of the invidivual in the American way of life, but he did not want this individual freedom to
enter his home. Ancient Rome flourished for centuries because of the Roman Legions that worked as one person,
thought Francesco, and this was the rule for the family whom
he and Maria had brought into the world. He was the patriarch
of the family, and from him must come all decisions for the ben-

efit of his children, until they matured and married and left his home.

Virgillia was their first child, born and educated in America. Now that she had reached her twentieth birthday, he and Maria wished she would marry one of their own country-men who had migrated to America, rather than have her play the field, especially since at the end of the First World War there was talk of Prohibition, where the speakeasy, the hip flask, and wild orgies would follow in its wake. Since the end of the war women were leaving the kitchens to become gainfully employed in expanding industries. The hemlines were shock-ingly raised up to the knees, and women began to shear their beautiful tresses, emerging with mannish haircuts. Women weighed heavily on Francesco's mind this morning. He had five daughters to marry. Where would he find five more good, solid men like his two sons-in-law?

Virgillia looked across the smudgy court as Francesco pointed with his toe wherever he spotted a pea for Tommy to pick up. Virgillia could see Tom Mulvaney shaving from a mir-ror that he had placed against his kitchen window. She lifted strands of curly black hair above her ears and slowly braided them. Her rounded breasts, tapering waist, and comely length of hips were revealed beneath the flimsy voile night-gown. The light ecru lace edging accented the coloring of her skin, matching it to the soft petals of a tea rose. Tom Mulvaney had the features of a bull, yet his skin was soft. Virgillia won-dered why he shaved. His smile was divine and his white teeth shone like pearls. Strange that she should like Donald's serious smile when she had thrilled to Tom's bright, happy face, she mused.

The door suddenly opened and Rosalia, Virgillia's oldest sister who lived on the floor below, entered, dragging her two children, Nicky and Nanny. Their faces were tear smudged, but they were now quietly sucking sticks of licorice. She loosened her hold of them and they squatted on the uncarpeted floor. For a second Rosalia stood with her hands on her hips viewing the scene before her. Quickly she picked up the strands of disorder.

"Pa, Virgillia is standing there almost naked making eyes at Tom Mulvaney, and you and ma are in the kitchen and you don't see her. Are you all going mad?" Virgillia turned quickly around and almost upset the pot with the peas again.

Maria gave her a shove saying, "Virgillia, you're standing in the way of the peas."

Rosalia tucked wisps of hair into her huge, curly bun as her mother spoke petulantly. Rosalia sensed her father's defeat in trying to make Virgillia into a pattern of herself and her sister Luisa. Perhaps he was getting older and needed her help in disciplining the younger children, she thought aggressively.

Now Francesco was busily straightening the stained mirror on the front wall of the kitchen between the two windows that faced the court. He felt piqued at Rosalia's reproof that he was being lax with Virgillia. Sometimes Rosalia, who Francesco was proud to admit was a capable wife and mother, seemed to forget that she too was still his daughter and subject to his will, even though he was glad that she took an avid interest in the problem, which was Virgillia. Through with adjusting the mirror, he moved aside and saw the reflection of Tommy tightening her nightgown around her childish figure, while making arched faces at herself. Before she could recover her own facial epression, Francesco caught her ear and gave her a shaking.

"That's enough acting, Tommy. Get dressed at once! Virgillia, why aren't you dressed. Where are your sisters, Bettina, Angie, and Caterina! See that you let Rosalia buy your next nightgown, Virgillia." He pointed at her nightgown with his hammer. "That one is much too thin."

Francesco was still smarting from Rosalia's implication

that he and Maria were getting too lenient with the children. He had taught Rosalia and Luisa that children should be seen and not heard. Of course Rosalia was too clever not to be heard, but not above him.

"Pa, everyone is wearing this kind of nightgown." Virgillia looked with shocked surprise from pa to Rosalia. "I bought it in one of the large stores near my office. They carry the latest styles. I didn't pick it from the pushcharts on Orchard Street." Virgillia hoped she could make her father perceive that during the past twenty years since he had migrated from Italy, the woman's liberation movement was on the move.

"Don't be ungrateful for the bargains mama picks on Orchard Street, Virgillia. The pushcart peddlars buy the latest styles from bankrupt businesses, but they won't buy see-through nightgowns for the good mothers and wives who shop along the street," informed pa.

"Maria, open your trousseau trunk and show the girls what you wore when you were a young girl." Maria looked up, then quickly cast down her eyes, flushing and smiling placidly to herself.

"Linen, Virgillia, ma wore linen pantelettes with wide edgings of lace that she crocheted herself instead of making eyes at strange men shaving in their undershirts across the court." Francesco, carried away by his description, flung his arms wide to emphasize the length of strings.

"Franci," Maria shook her head negatively, "be careful of what you say before the Madonna." Maria raised her eyes to the large colored picture of the Madonna Della Civita, which hung over the old sewing machine stacked with unpressed laundry. The Madonna had appeared centuries before in their Italian village of Itri on the outskirts of Rome. A dumb shepherd had first seen her apparition. Regaining his speech, he excitedly told the villagers what he had seen. To commemorate the spot, the villagers built a monastery there, which still stands today. The Vinas laid all their problems before their blessed Mother.

At Maria's word pa coughed, a trifle disconcerted, giving the beautiful Madonna an embarrassed sidelong glance.

"Pardon me, Madonna mia," he spoke softly, then turned to Virgillia.

"Tom Mulvaney is through shaving, Virgillia. Now you may get some clothes on." His voice was edged with sarcasm.

"It's about time, pa, you told her to get dressed," mumbled Rosalia resentfully, remembering the way she and Luisa had to be on their toes getting the younger children ready for school during the week and prepare them for mass on Sunday mornings.

To cover his lapse of discipline before Rosalia, Francesco now raised his voice.

"Virgillia, get the children ready for mass at once!"

Virgillia remembered she had a date with her girl friend Greta. She had almost forgotten it and the morning was going fast. She returned to the bedroom and tickled her sister Bettina's foot. Bettina opened blue, starry eyes.

"Sweet innocence," Virgillia teased amiably, flinging a pair of stockings at her.

"Bettina, please dress the children and take them to church for me today. I'm giving you a pair of new stockings. I'll go to a later mass. I had some trouble with Tommy, and it is getting late for me to do all the things I planned to do."

Bettina now fully awake regarded Virgillia thoughtfully.

"Hurry, Bettina, I want to visit Greta this afternoon, and I want to have time to make myself pretty. We are going to a dance." Virgillia examined her negligee, looking for a rip in the sleeve. Bettina surmised the trouble.

"Tommy, why don't you let Virgillia's things alone. She works hard enough to get them," defended peace-loving Bettina.

9

"Oh, quiet, pussyfoot! Just because you're next in line for her things, naturally you don't want me to use them." Tommy stuck out her tongue at Bettina, who ignored her. Virgillia gently awoke Angie and Caterina while Virgillia ceased to mind Tommy as she folded the bedding, straining her ears to catch the whisperings from the kitchen.

She saw Rosalia sitting opposite her mother, helping her shell peas. Her heavy set muscular body was wrapped in an old rose kimono, which was decorously pinned at the bottom with a huge blanket pin. Rosalia believed in teaching her sisters by practicing the modesty she preached.

"There is no end to these peas, ma," she said. Maria panted. The morning was going fast. "Anything could happen," dutiful Maria would proudly tell her neighbors, "but Francesco must have his dinner on the dot of one o'clock."

On Sunday morning, she and Francesco would arise at four-thirty as they used to do in their native village. At five o'clock they would go to church and at six o'clock Maria and Francesco would return home to start the chores, which the children would finish when they awakened.

Francesco now sat by the kitchen window examining the children's shoes. He had time to sole a few before the girls dressed.

Nicky and Nanny were stretched out on the kitchen floor, kicking their feet and giggling with licorice stuck between their teeth.

Rosalia moistened her thick lips and moved her chair closer to her mother. She shifted her black, slightly bulging eyes from mother to father.

"Pa, what are you going to do with Virgillia?" she scolded in a loud whisper. "Yesterday she was sitting on the stoop close to that Mulvaney boy. This morning she was making eyes at him across the court almost in the nude."

Francesco shook his sandy head dolefully as he placed

some tacks in his mouth before hammering them into the shoe before him.

"Franci, what has happened to our good friends, Salvatore and Luigi, who introduced Rosalia and Luisa to their husbands?"

"Ma, I've been begging pa to find them but he doesn't listen to me. If we wait much longer, Virgillia will join the suffragette movement, fall in love with some shiftless man, and then it will be too late." Rosalia finished ominously, shaking her heavy shoulders and settling her head back, challenging her father with battling eyes.

Francesco, hammering the last tack into the shoe, put down his hammer, then circling his thumb and forefinger, he explained patiently, "How many times must I tell you, Rosalia, that I have asked everyone I know of the whereabouts of Salvatore and Luigi. No one seems to know where they went. Some say they are living in Rhode Island where many of our countrymen migrated at the turn of the century." Exasperated, Francesco waved his thumb and forefinger up and down. "In Italy, in my village, boys and girls fell in love and married. In New York City I must get a salesman to have my daughters meet and marry men of Italian background," sighed Francesco dismally.

"Franci, it is a sacrilege to call Salvatore and Luigi salesmen. Sometimes you don't make sense, Franci! They knew we had two good daughters, Rosalia and Luisa, and they introduced the girls to two good men who fell in love with our daughters."

"What can I do to remind these good men, Salvatore and Luigi, that I have five more daughters, Maria? Besides, I don't know where to find them!" Francesco's voice edged irritably.

"Pa, with Virgillia's type girl you must take the bull by the horns. You must ask Salvatore and Luigi outright if they know of a nice boy who would make Virgillia a good husband. You can say, pa, 'My good friends, do you know that I have a daughter

11

who is twenty years old?' " Rosalia shook her heavy shoulders, settling her head back as was her habit when challenging her father in discussing his family problems.

"Rosalia, pa must use his head," Maria said slowly. "Salvatore and Luigi may say, 'What do we care that you have a daughter of twenty,' and the discussion might end right there. Either pa tells them that he wants a husband for Virgillia at once, otherwise he shouldn't open his mouth and make a fool of himself."

Francesco shook his head negatively as he looked at the old shoe before him.

"First I must find Salvatore and Luigi. Remember that, women. And then I must find a simpler method of approach to get them interested in Virgillia. They like feasting and weddings where the wine flows freely. Perhaps, if they see me, they'll remember the two weddings they enjoyed so much with us and they'll remember that we have five more unmarried girls at home," said Francesco hopefully.

Virgillia, with Bettina's help and Tomasina's disgruntled assistance, had rolled the huge mattress and placed it on Maria's trousseau trunk. Anxious to hear the hushed conversation in the kitchen, Virgillia impatiently quieted the children's voices as they told each other how it was best to hold one end of the mattress as Virgillia propelled it onto the trunk. Once it fell, almost smothering Angie and Caterina, Virgillia dismantled the ingenious bed which Francesco had made for his ever increasing family. The bed consisted of five boards a foot and a half wide, five and a half feet long which were nightly placed across two wooden saw horses. Virgillia now shooed the children into the parlor where they dressed and one by one she placed the boards behind the bedroom door. With the large bed out of the way, there was more room for the children to play on rainy days.

As the loud whispered words floated to her in the bedroom, she hoped fervently that Salvatore and Luigi would find themselves at the bottom of the Black Sea. She chose the Black Sea because the color matched her mood, she thought. Why did Rosalia have to meddle in her affairs? It was kind of Rosalia to willingly help ma with her large family, but no one was going to pick a husband for her, bristled Virgillia. If pa was afraid to have her mingle with people of other races because he did not understand them, then he should have remained in Italy. Pa was being very unreasonable, because in Italy she could fall in love with an Italian of low character. There were good and bad people in all racial groups. Pa was just being plain prejudiced.

Tommy's black oxfords, which had seen better days, tattooed impatiently as she tried to coax a wisp of flaxen hair into a six on her forehead. To do the trick she had to use saliva and had almost plastered it into submission when she felt a resounding slap on her cheek.

"What did I do? What did I do?" wailed Tommy defensively as she quickly tucked the strand of hair under one of Virgillia's discarded berets. Francesco was determined to prove to Rosalia the severity of his discipline with his younger daughters. Sometimes Rosalia did meddle too much in his family problems, thought Francesco, as he put away his cobbler's foot in his workbox under the table, looking sternly at Tommy, until she loosened her green coat which she was holding closely wrapped around her childish figure.

"Remember! You are only thirteen and have a long time in which to grow up, Tomasina!" Every child in a family has a different temperament, he thought. Aloud he said, "Virgillia doesn't want to grow up and Tomasina can't wait to do so." Francesco looked in the mirror and imitated Tommy. "She is already with the lipstick and the hairdo." Francesco tried to make a six with a strand of hair on his forehead. Maria rolled back her head and laughed. She knew Francesco had a kind heart, but the girls did try his patience. He had to be harsh at times. Maria glanced at the Madonna. "Dear Blessed Mother," she prayed silently, "tell your son Jesus to offer our love to God." The sunlight streaming through the window brightened the Madonna's face and Maria knew she was smiling.

"Virgillia!" Francesco's voice now bellowed through the railroad flat.

Virgillia hurried to the kitchen buttoning her blue cotton dress.

"What is it father?" Annoyance reflected in a pained expression looked through large, black eyes.

"O deah fawther," mimicked Tommy as she ran out of the kitchen with one of Rosalia's discarded pocket books swinging on her arm.

"Shall I buy two quarts of milk, fawther?" Outside the kitchen door, she circled her mouth with her hand, saying, "Rosalia, Virgillia got that fawther stuff from the movies." Virgillia slammed the door shut with the heel of her shoe. Rosalia laughed aloud. Francesco continued to put his tool box in order, saying, "Virgillia, are Bettina, Caterina, and Angelina dressed and ready for mass?"

"Bettina is taking them to the nine o'clock mass, pa. I'll go later. I must help ma cook the tomato sauce for the spaghetti."

"Virgillia, if you don't arise earlier to take the children to the nine o'clock mass so you'll have plenty of time to help ma make the tomato sauce for the spaghetti you'll have to come with me and ma to the five o'clock mass on Sunday morning, then you'll have plenty of time to help ma. I'll teach you to mind!"

"Shh, Franci, shh." Maria admonished Francesco when he warmed to a lengthy lecture. God had made men supreme. Secretly Maria liked to feel the weight of his discipline, knowing he was a just man. She remembered when Virgillia was born, the first daughter born in America. She was frightened alone in a new world without friends or relatives. Francesco had been tender, kind.

14

"Maria! That is how you spoil the children. You make them believe they are right when they are wrong." He flashed sharp, blue eyes from Maria to Virgillia. Virgillia busily turned her attention to the children's breakfast, pouring milk into the cereal filled bowls.

"Pa, I'll help ma with the tomato sauce this morning," offered Rosalia. Pa nodded wearily.

"After you wash the breakfast dishes Virgillia, you may go down to my flat and see what Rollo is doing. I left him sleeping in the crib. Don't forget to tidy up my place before you go to mass. I'll help ma with dinner."

Rosalia's buck teeth shone aggressively as she bustled around the kitchen. She wanted Virgillia out of the way so she could again coax pa to find Salvatore and Luigi to get Virgillia a husband. She noticed with a perturbed crease in her forehead that Virgillia was dressing more and more scandalously. That blue dress was so very snug, showing her well rounded breasts and hips. No wonder Tom Mulvaney rode with her to work on the streetcar every morning.

Maria had finished shelling peas. She got up slowly, heavily, dropping the shells to the floor and plodded to the iron sink with the pot of peas.

"Ma, don't hold the pot so close to your new dress. You'll stain it." Rosalia swept the pea shells into a dust pan admiring the black-and-white polka-dotted dress she had made for her mother by cutting a large neckline and stitching the dress down the sides. Maria gingerly held the pot away from her dress. Francesco looked at Maria and saw the new dress for the first time. He smiled approvingly on Maria and Rosalia. Rosalia was a clever daughter. He looked up at the Madonna and smiled gratefully.

TWO

Before going to Rosalia's flat on the third floor, Virgillia sat on the top step of their fourth floor hallway and stared at the weather-stained skylight. The Vinas had inhabited the four railroad rooms on the right side of the hall for the past twenty years. Virgillia was born there, one week after the Vinas arrived from Italy, at the turn of the century.

The yellow sunrays pouring from the skylight revealed the aged walls of the hallway. Virgillia liked sitting on the top step of the battered stairway of the tenement that had always been home to her. She liked to think of the remote era when the rickety halls with their knotty floors and mahogany bannister had glistened with newness. The section of Manhattan where the tenement was located had been an exclusive residential area a century before. Virgillia saw in her mind's eye beautiful girls stepping lightly, heard the swish of satin, the crackling of taffeta, drank the odor of many perfumes. She always figured largely in these daydreams and wondered if her lover would also mount these stairs, as lovers had done a century before and find her, Virgillia Vina, in the busy, crowded Vina flat. A month before she thought he would have a divine smile and pearly teeth like Tom Mulvaney. Now the picture changed. Would he have deep, violet eyes and a serious smile like Donald Long, the new man in the office?

Tommy's clattering oxfords running upstairs broke rudely on her fancies. Virgillia descended slowly to Rosalia's flat. Tommy raced past her.

"Hurry, Tommy, or you'll be late for the nine o'clock mass." Tommy grimaced. "I'd rather go to a later mass. Who wants to sit with all those babies at the children's mass?" Tommy argued with herself as she ran upstairs, the big, old pocketbook swinging crazily at her side.

Virgillia let herself in Rosalia's flat and locked the door. The quiet was keenly satisfying after the bustling in the Vina household. Rollo was crowing contentedly in his white crib by the kitchen window. Virgillia hugged him and he smiled with his toothless gums. Gently she put him back in the crib. He is quiet like his father Giuseppe, Virgillia thought kindly. She was glad to be alone. From the depths of the bedroom closet Virgillia took a soft, yellow gown trimmed with tulle. She opened a lower drawer of the bedroom dresser and took out a pink, silk chemise, a pair of sheer stockings, a net brassiere, and a white handkerchief on which she had crocheted a lace edging. Rosalia allowed Virgillia to store her best lingerie in her dresser drawer away from the prying children.

Once a month her friend Greta would get tickets for a Broadway play from her father. He had a poster advertising the latest shows in the window of his tailor shop, on upper Broadway, for which he received two free passes to the theater. Whenever Greta invited Virgillia to see a play it became a great event to Virgillia who had spent all of her twenty years close to Vina flat. With the many mouths to feed, Virgillia did not have much money left, after contributing most of her salary to her family, to spend in the entertainment spots of the city. Virgillia liked to be part of the large crowds moving along Broadway, seeking an evening's entertainment. Deep within her heart she knew she was a victim of her parent's migration to America. Her parents were latter-day pilgrims who came to struggle, to exist, to bring children into a new free land with opportunities for all. What the opportunities were for her, Virgillia could not understand, deprived of her salary, deprived of her right to fall in love with whom she pleased. Tonight, however, would be a surcease from her frustrations. She and Greta were not going to see a play. Greta's cousin had invited them to his neighborhood club dance.

Virgillia heard the tramp of feet descending, the loud shrill voices of the children quarreling over some triviality and then quiet again. She was glad they had gone to church without knocking on the door asking to see baby Rollo. Her mother's loud, contented voice ran through the court singing an Italian ditty, fitting her own words to the tune and when at a loss for words, substituting a deep, sonorous Ahhhhh. Virgillia often wondered how her mother so quickly improvised rhymes for her tunes when she could neither read or write.

Putting Rosalia's rooms in order was easy. Aside from the baby's crib, which was white, Rosalia had furnished her flat in maple furniture because imitation maple was cheaper than other grains of wood. Virgillia like it because it was neat and simple. Rosalia was a good manager of time and money, thought Virgillia admiringly, considering all the time she devoted to ma's large family, her clothes were neatly folded in the dresser drawers and her closets were in order. Rollo continued to gurgle in defiance of Francesco's strong voice, which floated down the court. No doubt, he was discussing some petty matter with Rosalia. Virgillia hoped the neighbors wouldn't think that pa and Rosalia were quarreling. Rosalia and pa were the most articulate members of the family, and they always found some subject to spar about. When the discussion at hand would become interminable, Maria would throw up her hands, take out her rosary and say, "If you would turn that chatter into prayers, you would save your souls." Silently she would finger the beads, but Francesco then would take Maria to task. One day after Maria's statement, he picked up an old picture frame from his workbox and squeezed it a little.

"You see, Maria, now the frame isn't a square anymore. When Rosalia and I discuss a subject, we only try to square the matter. We try to see it from a right perspective." He would

18

then push the frame back to its perfect square and return it to his workbox where he kept odds and ends.

"But, Francesco, not everyone sees with the same light of reasoning," Maria would say wisely, to which thought Francesco would nod dolefully.

Virgillia, in Rosalia's apartment, now placed the tea kettle on the gas burner. Through necessity she had learned to be her own beautician, clipping beauty hints from newspapers and pasting them in a scrap book. During 1920 the cosmetic companies would send free samples of face creams, lipstick, and rouge. Virgillia had a shoebox where she kept all her samples. Today she would give herself a mud pack. Of course, pa said that youth is beauty, but Virgillia did not agree with him. She had read that cosmetic firms earned millions of dollars yearly. That must mean that there weren't too many beautiful women, she reasoned with the naivete of youth. She set her wavy ringlets carefully. Pa did not even approve of bobbed hair, which more and more women were accepting. He said his daughters would have to keep their crowning glory until they were safely married. Bobbed hair went with hip flasks and the Charleston dance. Men who had migrated from his hometown might get the wrong impression of Vigillia if she cut her hair. They would think she was "fast" and she would lose her chance of matrimony. The world had been good until after the First World War. Everything was now going topsy-turvy. Women were forgetting their dignity with their short hair and hemlines over the knees, holding hands in public and dancing wildly, hugging each other closely. Everyone blamed it on Prohibition, but Francesco who had been raised in a wine-making country did not think it wrong for anyone to take a nip to circulate the blood. Prohibition only challenged youngsters to drink more than was good for them.

Virgillia had an artful way of letting her curly hair fall above her shoulders.

She now heard the thunderous peals of the church gongs and gasped. The Roman Catholic church was located around the corner from the old tenement in which the Vinas lived. Its steeple adorned with a huge clock towered over the roofs of the sooty tenements.

She picked one of Rosalia's discarded turbans, covered her curlers, and hurried to church. She might have time for her mud pack after mass, she thought, but no sooner did she return to Rosalia's flat, than she heard her name floating down the court.

"Virgillia, Virgillia!" Rosalia's imperious voice calling out of the window told Virgillia that it was time for her to set the table for dinner. Time went so quickly when she awoke late that she barely had time for her own personal needs, she thought impatiently.

Setting the table for the Vinas was a herculean task. Francesco, Maria, Virgillia, Bettina, Tommy, Angie, Caterina, Rosalia, Giuseppe, Nicky, Nanny, and Rollo. Rollo would rest on Maria's big, brass bed, all demanding attention. Virgillia always murmured a silent prayer when a flat vacated in the tenement, and Maria asked hopefully if Luisa would be interested in moving from the Bronx where she lived. Fortunately for Virgillia, Luisa's in-laws had dug their roots deep in the Bronx, and Luisa was happy there, near her husband's family.

Virgillia had finally dragged the last chair to its respective place around the table. It was the children's task to assemble the chairs, but Virgillia found it easier to do it herself today than round up the scattered children.

At one o'clock sharp the family gathered for the much prepared Sunday dinner. Rosalia set the large platter with spaghetti in the center of the table. Today she had surprised her family by making her favorite mushroom tomato sauce. She felt repaid when the children murmured a delighted

Mmmmmmmmmm when they spotted the mushrooms decorating the spaghetti.

There was a moment of silence as Francesco quietly crossed himself and said grace, then he served Maria and himself. Giuseppe took care of his family, while Virgillia heaped her sisters' dishes with spaghetti.

"I—I don't want any," stuttered six-year-old Angie.

"If you aren't hungry, leave the table," ordered Francesco, holding his fork against the spoon as he rolled the spaghetti around the fork. The children giggled. Everyohe knew that Angie preferred the meat dishes. Angie slowly toyed with her fork, then began to eat. If she had to get to the meat she knew she had no choice but to eat the spaghetti. Bettina covertly signaled Virgillia with her fingers for the small portion she desired. Caterina ate eagerly, looking neither to the right nor left.

Virgillia hoped the family would finish dinner early. She wished to see Greta at two o'clock.

"Pa, are you making new wine this fall?" asked Giuseppe as he soaked the tomato sauce off his dish with a crust of Italian bread.

"Giuseppe, it's too early even to think of new wine and grapes," said Rosalia with a trace of annoyance. Rosalia habitually overruled her husband, but Giuseppe, a short, stocky man with a round, kind face and lazy brown eyes, did not care whether she did or not. Rosalia had married him, encouraged him to open a shoe shine parlor, and tried to solve every problem he brought home.

"It isn't too early to talk about making new wine, Rosalia. We've always made it before our neighbor Signora Derella, and I'll see that we'll be the first ones to make wine this fall too." Francesco brought his fist down on the table. The glasses and dishes tinkled.

Virgillia, through with serving the children, sat down, glad that the conversation had turned to wine making instead of the problem of finding her a husband. The Sunday meal was the only meal that Rosalia and Giuseppe enjoyed with the Vinas, giving the elders a chance to better discuss vital matters.

"If we're careful with the wine," Giuseppe was saying quietly, "we won't have to make any this year." Rosalia and Giuseppe paid half the cost for the grapes, and when Francesco found himself without funds, which was quite often, they usually paid the entire bill. The muscle of Francesco's lean jaw bulged, as Giuseppe finished speaking, a sure sign of battle, thought peace-loving Giuseppe, who quickly added, "We can buy the grapes late in the autumn, pa, and get them cheaper."

"Must we show our neighbors that we cannot afford to make new wine?" asked Francesco proudly. Autumn was a difficult time for Francesco in the new world of America, for in Italy it was the time of year ushering the wine making season with gayety and laughter.

"Povero, Francesco," thought Maria. Her heart too yearned to be with the wine festival in her native village. It had been fun to dance the tarantella on the village square, dressed in native costume, while decorated wagons full of grapes paraded the streets, the wine flowing freely from door to door. She knew Francesco didn't care as much about his neighbors as he wanted to get his hands into the grapes and feel he was part of the wine festival across the ocean.

Rosalia wanted to challenge Francesco, saying, "Let's face it, pa, can we really afford new wine with so many mouths to feed and cloth?" but she glanced at ma and saw the longing expression in her eyes for their merry way of life in Italy and bit her tongue remorsefully.

"All right, then we won't make wine," said Francesco with sudden finality, "as long as it makes Giuseppe and Rosalia happy!"

Maria had been slowly eating. Now she laid her fork on her plate.

"Mama mia, Franci," she exclaimed, wiping her chin with a huge red and white checkered napkin, "we have always had wine on the table since we came to America. Does it matter when we make it, Franci," she soothed, trying to assuage his hurt feelings. "Virgie, bring the second course to the table. Maybe the cutlets will make pa feel better." When it comes to wine making, thought Maria affectionately, he is like a child. Doesn't he understand that the cost may be too much for Rosalia and Giuseppe?

"Mbeh, in my own home I have to be told when to make wine." Francesco shook his head sadly as he refilled his wine glass and gulped it down. Wine and spaghetti didn't taste well together. With the meat dishes, it blended better. We never drank wine after spaghetti in Italy, he thought. Sometimes Rosalia confused him with her constant chattering.

"Let's hope that Virgillia or Bettina will marry within the year, pa, then we'll have a good excuse to make new wine and we'll make it early, even if we have to get into debt," said peace-loving Giuseppe. All eyes turned to Virgillia who studied her cutlet with undue attention.

"Eek-ou-ouch!" Tommy crouched back in her chair, covered her head with her hands and screamed frantically as Bettina flushed with anger pinched her arm. Bettina was Francesco's pet daughter. Rarely aroused she gave Francesco least cause for worry, but now two red patches appeared on her rounded cheeks.

"Pa, Tommy stole my silk stockings. The pair that Virgillia gave me this morning." Bettina caught Tommy's shoulder and shook her.

Virgillia marched Tommy to the parlor and sat her on the floor with a thud. Tommy looked at Virgillia through her widespread fingers and giggled.

"Bettina told you she didn't want too much spaghetti and you gave her more than you gave me, so there!" Tommy said defensively.

"You're a troublemaker." Virgillia gave her a shove.

"I don't care if I tore them. Bettina is only three years older than I am and she has silk stockings and all your hand-me downs. She just keeps them in her drawer but I—oh how I love swishy, silky things to wear!" Tommy passionately clutched her small hands to her breast. Tommy's emotional technique had acquired its finesse from the stolen hours she spent in the silent movies after school. She ran errands for the neighbors, jealously hoarding her pennies until she had the price of a movie admission.

"Act natural, Tommy, or pa will wonder why you're acting funny. He'll guess you go to the movies more than once a week." Virgillia had taken off her stockings and rolled them into a ball. "Go quietly and take my seat. I'll sit next to Bettina."

Virgillia sighed as she pushed Tommy ahead of her. Restlessly she glanced at the clock. It was half past one. Her appointment with Greta was for two o'clock. Francesco had made light of Tommy's quarrel with Bettina. He was used to the girls' wrangling over stockings and petticoats. Francesco never rushed his Sunday dinner which Maria, with the help of her daughters, prepared with such care. Marriage had given Francesco a sense of life's completeness such as he had never felt in his bachelor days. It didn't matter, he often thought, if a man was rich or poor, intelligent or ignorant, a man could be king on his own level with a wife and children to love him to the end of his days. Marriage made life complete for most men and women and that is why he wanted to see Virgilia married. Marriage to Francesco meant stability, just as a steamer anchored in port and he did want all his daughters well anchored.

Francesco sighed with satisfaction. The spaghetti sauce was good. The cutlets were tender and well browned, just the way he liked them. The broccoli salad, dressed with olive oil, minced garlic and lemon juice, tantalized his taste buds, and the wine which he and Giuseppe made was rare. Indeed it was a splendid dinner, and he did not hesitate to compliment Maria and Rosalia. He even had to admit that Giuseppe helped him make good wine. It was his young strength that squeezed the last bit of juice from the grapes when he danced on them in his clean, bare feet in the cellar below the tenement.

"The wine helps digest the food." Maria would coax the children to sip a bit of wine poured into their glasses, the way her mother had made her sip hers in Italy when she was a little girl. Drinking quarts of milk in Italy was unheard of, the fat of the milk lay like lead in your veins, but the good wine circulated the bloodstream, thought Maria, for these were the precepts on which she had been bred.

Virgillia poked Bettina.

"Help me with the dishes," she whispered, "Greta and I are going to a dance."

"Let Tommy help you. Didn't she take my stockings? I'll scrape the dishes, put them on the drainboard, and sweep the floor."

Tommy heard Virgillia's whisper and Bettina's answer. She was glad to make amends with Bettina, who was usually easygoing. Stockings tore easily. They were expensive and she could not blame Bettina for complaining this afternoon. Tommy took a fair view of Bettina's decision concerning the dishes.

"Caterina, you wipe!" ordered Tommy loudly.

"Wipe what?" Caterina, usually in her own world of thought, looked bewildered.

"The dishes, of course," Tommy stated loudly.

"I won't!" flared quiet Caterina with unusual spirit. Her thin face flushed resentfully. She was tall for her twelve years, as tall as Tommy, only as Virgillia said, Caterina acted her age. It was Caterina's duty to keep an eye on chubby Angie. Caterina liked to play with dolls and read fairy tales and Angie appreciated both. Tommy had never played with dolls and didn't like fairy tales. Life in its reality was exciting enough for Tommy. Yet as clever as Tommy was, she never seemed to understand that Caterina was blessed with two natures, the dreamy side of her and the very much down to earth Caterina who wasn't going to let Tommy get away with anything.

"I'm thirteen and I wipe dishes. You're twelve, just right to learn!" With the corner of her sharp blue eyes, Tommy saw her father weighing the situation. Although Tommy knew that pa respected book learning up to a point, he always stressed the fact that a woman had to first learn the duties of a housewife.

Virgillia frowned at Tommy as she wiped Angie's chin. Rosalia in a hushed tone was talking to Giuseppe about the wine making. Maria sat relaxed in her chair. Whenever her eyes strayed to the Madonna she said a silent prayer, such as make Francesco's burden light or take care of my daughters, Madonna mia, in this strange, new land. Maria had the simple faith of her forebears. Life became less complex when she placed her thoughts with the Madonna and when she had a burden she would place it in the hands of Her Son, Jesus, for He said, "Come to me ye who are heavy burdened and I will give you rest."

"Pa, Caterina and Angie have to go to catechism class this afternoon," reminded Virgillia.

Tommy's heart beat fast at Virgillia's words. To Maria and Francesco, God was the reality of life, for life in this world was not forever, yet the soul of man lived on forever. Tommy knew that religion was more important to pa than wiping dishes, even though he expected his daughters to be good housewives. Under the circumstances would pa prefer Caterina to wipe dishes or arrive at Sunday school on time?

"Work fast and you'll get to Sunday school on time," Francesco said slowly. The verdict was better than Tommy anticipated. She hastily blew her nose to smother a victorious smile. As soon as the incident was forgotten Tommy glanced at Caterina who looked at her defiantly. Only Caterina noticed Tommy sticking two fingers above the table. Caterina knew that that meant she needed two pennies to go to the movies and she would wipe the dishes if Caterina was willing to give them to her. Caterina's large brown eyes looked at her disdainfully as she said loud enough for all to hear, "Tommy, don't think you're a smarty. I'll wipe dishes but I won't give you two cents to send you to the movies." Tommy flushed. Virgillia laughed aloud.

"Good work, Caterina," she said.

Francesco looked narrowly at Tommy. Maria shook her head sadly. "Tommy, I'll have to speak to Father Ignatius about you."

"Ma, I haven't said a word, honest, I haven't," said Tommy defensively.

"Actions speak louder than words, Tommy," said Virgillia as she arose, tweaking her ear. It was getting late and she had to go to Greta at two o'clock.

After the small glass of wine, Maria felt drowsy. Her head rested on her right shoulder. Rosalia, Giuseppe, and Francesco lingered at the table, crunching celery dipped in olive oil, sprinkled with salt and black pepper. Bettina disappeared with Rollo to Rosalia's apartment. She would put the baby to sleep and then make herself comfortable with a book in Rosalia's parlor. Caterina and Angie having wiped the dishes had gone to Sunday school while Tommy folded the unpressed clothes on the sewing machine, under pa's watchful eyes.

"Tommy, I don't want to see any unpressed clothes in the room on Sunday," Francesco ordered, hoping that work would keep Tommy from mischief.

"All right, pa," Tommy answered meekly. She would be good for a while, she promised herself. She wasn't too anxious to have a heart to heart talk with Father Ignatius, her Sunday school teacher. He seemed to be waiting for her weekly confession to give her the stiff penance of praying a whole rosary for two days.

Virgillia fingered the tablecloth nervously. Would the crunching of celery never cease? She was a grown woman, she worked to help support ma and pa's large family, why couldn't she be a person and live her own life. Inwardly Virgillia knew the answer, this is the way families lived in Italy and ma and pa didn't know any other way. She felt in bondage to her family.

"I want to clear the crumbs off the tablecloth, pa. I have an appointment."

"Sunday is a family day, a day of rest, Virgillia."

Virgillia stamped her foot impatiently. Pa seemed to have the tentacles of a cuttlefish the way he drew his children to himself, regardless of age, she thought irritably. She and Greta had so many things to discuss this afternoon.

"You see, pa, Virgillia leaves earlier every Sunday. If you would only find Luigi and Salvatore, they might have a nice boy for her, and then she will be too busy to run to Greta." When Rosalia spoke hurriedly her buck teeth seemed larger.

"Mind your own business," mouthed Virgillia. Aloud she said, "Forget Luigi and Salvatore, Rosalia. I'll find my own husband, just like ma and pa found each other near the fountain in Italy."

Rosalia's mouth fell open at Virgillia's boldness.

"Pa, you don't know what is written in the newspapers these days. All the young boys and girls are carrying hip flasks and dancing the Charleston. They shake all over. If Virgillia goes with Greta, she'll be doing the same thing," cautioned Rosalia.

Giuseppe sat lazily back in his chair, his two hands in his pockets. He bent his head to look into the parlor. Nicky and Nanny were quietly playing with his hat.

"Does Greta expect you, Virgillia?" he asked quietly.

"Yes!" said Virgillia.

"It is all right if she goes, Pa Vina," Guiseppe said slowly. "When you find Luigi and Salvatore, it will be time enough for Virgillia to stay home and await her company." Rosalie bit her lips, her black eyes glared annoyingly at her husband for interfering with Virgillia's discipline.

"Do you remember, Pa Vina, the whiskey Greta's mother sent you when you had a bad cold last winter?" Giuseppe ignored Rosalia's stare. He liked peace and quiet and fair play.

"Mbeh, Giuseppe, if you think Virgillia should visit her friend on Sunday afternoon and leave her family before dinner is over, what can I say? In my own home I must be told how to raise my daughter—Mbeh!" Yes, thought Francesco anxiously, as he shrugged his shoulders, Rosalia was right. He had better find Luigi and Salvatore as soon as possible. Feeling inadequate, helpless in coping with Virgillia, he drained the wine from the bottle. He sensed the wondrous restlessness of this strange, great American country in which he and Maria had chosen to make their home and raise their children. Virgillia, his first American born daughter, seemed steeped with this restlessness. Life at the turn of the century had been quiet, staid, but now in the early twenties he felt the pulse of life accelerating. Where would it all end?

Virgillia quickly left the room before pa had a chance to put down the bottle, afraid he might change his mind about her leaving the family on Sunday.

Who cares about Luigi and Salvatore. They will never influence my life, thought Virgillia, yet Rosalia's determination in urging pa to locate the two old friends who would find her a husband gave her an uneasy feeling.

Francesco climbed on the fire escape. He poked around his garden boxes. Francesco loved the earth in the spring. He dug his hands in the black earth and imagined himself on his large farm in Italy.

Bettina had put Rollo to sleep. She lay curled up asleep on

Rosalia's sofa, her rosy cheek tucked in the crook of her arm, a book rested under her chin. Things seemed to come easy to Bettina. Would the world be kinder to Bettina because she took the path of least resistance? Virgillia wondered. She took off her slippers and walked cautiously in her stocking feet. Carefully she dressed. One of her nails caught in her sheer hose. She wet her thumb and pressed the pulled thread. The yellow tulle floated around her slim figure. Virgillia had bought the tulle for the plain yellow dress that Rosalia had given her for her birthday. She had sewed the tulle around the armhole and ruffled some at the bottom of the skirt. She had copied the idea from an exclusive dress shop window that featured the style, on one of her window shopping tours. She would spend the afternoon at Greta's flat. Greta was a beautician who would polish her nails and fix her hair. They would practice dance steps, then as the afternoon waned they would take a walk around the neighborhood and finally wind up the evening at Greta's cousin's dance club in the neighborhood.

THREE

Greta, large, blonde with plain features, greeted Virgillia with exciting news. "Dad got two tickets for the play *Glass Shutters*. The newspapers are raving about it. The tickets are for next Saturday. You better hold them, Virgillia. I'm always losing things, and these are too precious to lose."

She handed Virgillia the tickets, then added, "Will you be able to go, Virgillia?" Greta knew how difficult it was for Virgillia to detach herself from her family. When Greta discussed the Vina family with her mother she would say, "Those 'eyetalians' are queer in the head. I don't know why Francesco and Maria want to keep a strangle hold on Virgillia when they have four younger daughters and perhaps more coming." Greta and her mother laughed at the queer ways of the eyetalians.

"Guess what!" exclaimed Virgillia, then added before Greta answered, "Pa seemed more lenient today when I left earlier."

"Well, it's about time, Virgie. Your father must like having his women around," she chuckled.

"Now I have another problem," Virgillia's eyes were troubled. "You know that nosey body Rosalia is pushing pa to find Luigi and Salvatore, family friends who introduced husbands to her and Luisa. They are going to ask him to find a husband for me. Greta, that's what I call nerve, real nerve!" Virgillia stamped her foot and crinkled the sides of her nose.

"Virgillia, you won't see it in our generation but a time will come when young people coming of age will rent their own apartments away from their parents, so they can be themselves and not feel dominated like children, especially girls, if they don't marry."

"If I would be born fifty years from now I would still be

sucked in by my family, because they would need financial aid," said Virgillia hopelessly.

"I've read that in the future the government will give financial security to retired people and to those in need."

The girls fell silent. They were in Greta's bedroom. Greta was the only daughter of comfortable German immigrants. She had an oak bedroom set, plain and solid like herself. Virgillia sat before the sturdy vanity table with its hanging mirror. Greta polished Virgillia's nails and tweezed her eyebrows. She was a beautician and willingly offered her services to her friend.

"You have a widow's peak, Virgillia, but you don't show it off." Greta now looked thoughtfully at Virgillia.

"Tonight find a guy and fall in love on the spot. That will put a good crimp in Rosalia's plans," she suggested.

Greta fussed with Virgillia's hair, parting it in the center, accentuating the peak which dipped below the hair line, then she brushed the hair up from the temple and set the numerous black ringlets above small shapely ears.

"There, that looks better." They both looked in the mirror to study the effect. Virgillia smiled, pleased at her reflection. High rounded cheeks rose to meet curly eyelashes. The slight indentation in her full chin pressed itself upward forcing red lips to open gently.

"You do look ravishing, Virgillia."

"Thank you, Greta. Pa wouldn't approve of this getup," giggled Virgillia.

Francesco's voice floated down the court. That was how people hearing Francesco's voice knew that spring had arrived. His garden of mint and basilica plants in the wooden boxes grew large and substantial. As he tended them he spoke loudly enough for Maria to hear him in the kitchen. He became excited and eager as a child when he saw the seedlings sprout.

"Why does your father get so excited over those old garden boxes on the fire escape? Every spring we hear him shouting at them." Greta seemed puzzled. Virgillia giggled.

"The mint leaves ma uses to make a fish sauce with oil and vinegar and minced garlic which she sprinkles on some kinds of fried fish. Mint tastes good in a glass of cold lemonade or in a glass of red wine with slices of peach and an ice cube on hot summer days. The basil leaves sweeten the tomato sauce. Basil is a 'must' herb for an Italian tomato sauce."

"Different things make different people happy," said Greta with a shrug.

"It is getting late, Greta. Let's practice some dance steps." It wasn't long before Virgillia and Greta were wildly dancing the Charleston to the tune of the latest hit song.

Old brownstone houses on Seventh Street between First and Second Avenue served as club rooms or dance halls, hired for meetings or social gatherings during the early 1920s in Manhattan. The Ghetto Socialites were ushering spring with screeching jazz band and high spirits. Virgillia did not make scenery for the walls. She was caught, crushed, whirled in a frenzied exuberance of wild, animal gusto. Virgillia shut her eyes while dancing. She liked dancing. She wanted to dance. Her hand would slip from her partner's moist palm. The neighborhood boys cut into her dances. She wasn't surprised to meet Tom Mulvancy. On the streetcar one morning he had asked her to go to the dance with him. She had refused. She preferred meeting him there with Greta, then she didn't have to stay with him all evening. Now he held her closely as he danced, a bit too closely, thought Virgillia. He tried to kiss her. Virgillia avoided him with a laugh. Her smiling acquaintance she had with him when she met him going to work on the streetcar or when he sat with her on her stoop had served until now. Donald Long had opened a new vista for Virgillia. Now Virgillia knew that you could be attracted to more than one male. She knew now she must evaluate a man for his husband potential.

"Won't you be my steady date, Virgillia?" he pleaded. Tom had been drinking. He now shoved his flask to Virgillia's lips.

"I—I don't drink," stammered Virgillia.

"You're trying to pull the crinoline stuff, Virgillia. From my kitchen window I saw wine on your table. We're pals, just the same." He took another slug of liquor. "You'll take a drink by the time you're finished dancing with me."

Virgillia felt uncomfortable. She did not associate table wine with hard liquor. She danced in silence. Suddenly the dance hall filled with darkness. Someone in jest had turned off the lights. Loud screeches, sonorous yells, and yelping band music rent the air. Virgillia slipped out of the hall. She met Greta in the dressing room.

"How many men did you make, Virgillia?" Greta's light blue eyes were unusually bright with the excitement of the evening.

"None," said Virgillia shortly.

"Gee, you're a funny kid. I wish I had your looks."

"You did all right, Greta. I saw you dance every dance. Each one with a different fellow. Be careful, you might forget Pete."

Virgillia knew that Greta's boyfriend, Pete, who was making a career of army life, had given her permission to go to the neighborhood dances. Virgillia hoped her words had not sounded harsh, for Greta was her best friend. "If I were you, Virgillia, I would grab a guy before Rosalia finds you one of those 'eyetalians' right off the banana boat." Virgillia shrugged her shoulders.

"Come, let's get out of here. Let's go for a banana split." Virgillia led the way out of the dance hall.

Maria went to bed in the early hours of the morning. She took so many impromptu snoozes during the day that sleep did not come easily if she retired early.

Now she squatted in her favorite seat near the kitchen window opposite the Madonna. She was crocheting a bedspread with heavy ecru cotton. In her native Italian village, no trousseau was complete without a hand-crocheted bedspread. How else would a suitor know that he was marrying an industrious wife? In America girls didn't have time to sit and crochet a bedspread. When they were young they played with dolls and after they grew older, they went to school and then to work, Maria would say, and that is why she took it upon herself to crochet a bedspread for each one of her daughters, trying to coax them to lend her a hand on occasions.

Virgillia let herself in the kitchen quietly. It was much later than she had planned to return home.

"Is pa sleeping?" she whispered cautiously.

"What's the matter, Virgillia. Don't you see the time?" Maria pointed to the embroidered clock on the mantlepiece above the iron kitchen stove with her crochet needle. "Instead of helping on your bedspread the way Rosalia and Luisa used to do, you go out walking late at night." Maria's chubby fingers worked deftly as she spoke in low tones.

Virgillia wrinkled her forehead as she quickly took off her coat. Not talkative, Virgillia found that her mother in the quiet of the night found it easier to connect her thoughts. She hoped she could get to bed before their conversation awakened pa.

"Come here, Virgillia. I have something to tell you."

"What is it, ma?" Virgillia turned impatiently towards her mother.

"Virgie, come closer, Virgie." Her mother seemed to have a secret she wanted to share.

"Salvatore and Luigi are coming to see you. I knew pa would find them. They were surprised that you are twenty years old. Time flies. When Rosalia and pa make up their minds to do a thing, they usually do it." Maria rambled in a complacent whisper.

35

"I know they do," Virgillia muttered darkly. The dim gas light watched Virgillia's paling face.

"They said they will find you a nice boy, Virgillia."

"I don't want them to find me a nice boy, ma." Virgillia stamped her foot.

Maria chuckled to herself.

"That is right, Virgillia. That is the way to talk. I am glad that my daughter is so modest. It would not be right for you to speak differently at the beginning of a romance. You must never show a man you are too anxious."

Maria had forgotten to speak quietly. A slight cough from the first bedroom made Virgillia motion to her mother to be silent.

She was tired and exasperated at her mother's density and was not ready to discuss her romance with pa in the middle of the night.

A sense of helplessness surged through her. The wick in the red glass in the brass candelbra swinging before the Madonna sputtered and blew out. In the flickering light she caught the peaceful eyes of the Madonna, which seemed to look straight at her.

"Dear Madonna," Virgillia's heart prayed, "I want to fall in love and get married, but I don't want to be matched to a husband."

FOUR

It was a quarter to nine. The stenographic department was never still. When typewriters rested, voices buzzed.

"Returned home quite late." Virgillia finished her weekend recital.

"But aren't you going to see him again?" A girl asked as she applied her lipstick.

"I don't know." Virgillia dusted her desk as she spoke.

"Don't be silly, enjoy yourself before you settle down." The buzzer buzzed loudly.

"Miss Vina speaking," said Virgillia in her most businesslike tone.

"Miss Hawks wants to see you in her private office," came back the voice.

What had she done wrong? Virgillia wondered. Miss Hawks only called employees to her office when they were going to be discharged. She could not afford to lose her position. She went in panic to see Miss Hawks.

Virgillia was surprised. Virgillia's promotion had happened so suddenly.

"Remember, Miss Vina, perfection is his keynote."

"Yes, Miss Hawks, thank you."

Virgillia remembered well a conversation she had overheard. Speaking of a deficiency in one of the departments, Mr. Long had said, "No whole is complete without its component parts and no whole is perfect if one component part is imperfect. In order to have a one hundred percent firm, we must have every part to fit into the perfect whole." Virgillia had been impressed, even though the man with whom he was speaking had slapped his shoulder good humoredly when he finished his perfect little speech. She would be another spoke in his wheel of efficiency.

Virgillia felt a thrill of successful achievement with her promotion, which was multiplied when she found herself sitting side by side with Donald Long, sharing his large, private office. Her small mahogany desk next to his enormous one. The hero of her dreams became a reality.

Donald was telephoning when she entered his office. During his absence he had been busy and had given his closely written notes to his friend, Ben Worth, a squat, jovial fellow who gave them to Virgillia. He had recommended Virgillia to Donald Long.

"Donald, Miss Vina is just the secretary you need, capable intelligent, settled," he had said when Donald's secretary had left. He should have known Ben better, Donald thought ruefully. Even before he noted her stenographic pad and pencil in her hand he was startled by two large, limpid black eyes, staring at him, not brazenly but confidently.

He told Ben he preferred a mature, settled secretary, capable and unobtrusive. He looked into Virgillia's velvet eyes, dimpled chin, saw her shapliness. He could not account for his sense of gladness.

"How do you do, Miss Vina," he said briskly, pushing the telephone from him, holding her glance. "We will have to work very hard to make up my work that has fallen behind."

"I'm ready," said Virgillia, smiling as she sat before her desk, opening the drawers to find a place for her purse.

Virgillia had to make good her promotion, she thought as during the following week she plied Mr. Long with intelligent questions concerning his work, which she systematically took under control. Once during one particular morning she brought to his attention a minor error that he had committed. She laughed inwardly at the comic expression of disbelief on his lean face. Sheepishly he had smiled as he corrected it, his brow furrowed, wondering how it had occurred.

"The sun will hurt your eyes," he had said solicitiously as he drew the green shade, the intent dark blue eyes watching her as he slowly pulled the cord shading her eyes from the sun's glare.

The morning flew and afternoon found them again assiduously at work. At the end of the fifth day Donald pushed several architectual plans away from him and swung back in his swivel chair.

"We did very well." He smiled at Virgillia and again thought of mischievous Bob who knew of Donald's dislike of young, scatterbrained secretaries. Virgillia was capable as Bob had said but the world *settled* did not fit her.

"Don't you drink water?" asked Virgillia as she took out her purse from her desk drawer. "I drank three glasses of water today. You didn't get up once to take a drink."

"I'm like a camel. I carry water inside of me." His mouth opened to a wide grin, flashing strong, white teeth. It was kind of her to think of him, he thought as he slipped into his coat.

Virgillia liked the way he dressed in subdued colors. He brushed his hat with his hand. Taken apart, his features were not handsome for his mouth was too wide, his straight nose a bit short, but his high forehead, serious blue eyes, and sensitive chin appealed to Virgillia. Her face wreathed in a smile as she picked his muffler from the floor.

"Don't leave souvenirs for the porter, Mr. Long." She watched him as he put it around his neck folding it across his chest.

"If you wore it the other way, it would look sharper." Deftly she powdered her nose.

"Which way?" he asked, taken unawares at her simple familiarity.

Her slender fingers quickly knotted the scarf at his throat, then stood aside to study the effect. Donald untied the knot and folded it his accustomed way.

"I don't want to appear like a Beau Brummel, Miss Vina." They both laughed. His laugh ended in a smile. Virgillia liked his brooding smile.

Donald had been transferred from his Boston office to the Manhattan branch of the firm. As he turned homeword he thought of his bachelor quarters on Central Park West, where he lived with his friend Ben Worth. Ben had been a wonderful tonic for Donald since Margaret, his fiancée, had left him. Donald had met Margaret while employed in the Boston office, a girl architect with whom he fell in love, and just as he was about to propose, she received a telegram from Texas calling her home, for her mother was dying. After three months, she wrote Donald that she had met her childhood sweetheart, Doctor Blane, whom she married. She promised Donald she would visit him with Doctor Blane some time in the future.

After he lost his fiancée, Donald had felt depressed and disinterested in his former hobbies, which he had enjoyed with Ben Worth. Ben had introduced one or two of his girl friends to Donald, to turn his mind from Margaret, but Donald refused Ben's shot in the arm to perk his lost enthusiasm. It was Ben who planed back and forth to Boston, who suggested the New York transfer for his friend Donald. Donald promised himself when he took the position in New York that he would never again fall in love.

When Donald opened the door of his apartment, Ben greeted him with a sly smile. Donald was surprised to see Ben's latest attraction lanquishing on the oyster-colored satin couch. He and Ben had planned to see the play *Glass Shutters*. Stag.

"Meet Delight, Donald," Ben greeted cheerfully, then added, "she is a model."

"A home does need a cozy fire and a beautiful woman," Donald said dryly, wondering how Ben kept up with his steady stream of girls. It was off with the old and on with the new.

"Donald, I thought you would invite Miss Vina to see *Glass Shutters*. Can't you get in touch with her? Cocktails first, dinner, and then the play. You know where she lives."

"No, thank you Ben. I brought home some very important work from the office," Donald said curtly. Ben shrugged his shoulders, wrapping Delight in her silver fox cape.

The door closed on Ben and his date, who went to their cocktails giggling like two carefree teenagers.

Mandy, their maid, must have had a delicious roast in the oven for it smelled good, but Donald did not have too much appetite. As he took off his muffler he remembered Virgillia's soft voice saying, "If you put it the other way, it will look nicer." She had been thoughtful of him. He remembered Margaret had never watched the details of his dress. He shook his head as though with the movement he could discard his thoughts of Margaret. Why was he comparing Virgillia to Margaret? No, this would never do, he thought with alarm. He did not want to become involved with another woman so soon after his hurt. A few minutes later he was under the shower. It was a needle shower and it was cold. Had he put those architectural plans in his briefcase? They would keep him busy until bedtime.

FIVE

Virgillia's trip home was filled with thoughts of her new position. She had never expected to be promoted to private secretary so soon. It had been two years since Virgillia began working in her present office. She had started as mail clerk. After one year, she had been promoted to the stenographic department, knowing that with hard work she would advance to the position of private secretary. Coming unexpectedly the promotion materialized sooner than she had anticipated. Donald, who came with the promotion, left her breathless. Of course she had admired him from afar, so had the other ninety-nine girls in the stenographic department. She had had many doubtful moments, wondering if it was wise for her to dream of him, rather than set her cap for any nice young man who came on the floor, as did the other girls in the department. Whenever she thought of Donald, who she knew never noticed her as he hurried along the corridors, rapt in his own thoughts, she often thought of a poem she had learned in the elementary grades—"Why was I born to blush unseen and waste my perfume on the desert air?" The words would drum in her mind as she mechanically typed letters and reports day in and day out.

Now, as she approached the tenement in which she lived, Nicky and Nanny ran toward her, eager to give her the evening greeting of, "Give me a penny, Auntie Virgie, give me a penny." She tousled Nicky's chestnut hair and wiped Nanny's smooty chin.

"You need a bath and a penny," smiled Virgillia affectionately.

"No, no, I only need a penny," Nanny's round eyes followed Virgillia's fingers as they searched inside her purse.

"We had a bath. We didn't get a penny," informed Nicky with a wide grin.

"Did you eat your supper?" The children nodded. "Here's a penny for Nicky and a penny for Nanny. Buy chocolate." The children scampered to the candy store further down the street.

Caterina sitting on the stoop was reading a fairy tale to Angie. As soon as they spied Virgillia, they ran toward her.

"Giuseppe is very sick, Virgillia. Rosalia hopes he doesn't have to go to the hospital," informed Caterina sadly.

"Rosalia is crying." Angie wiped her own tears as she spoke.

"What is the matter with him?" Giuseppe just could not afford to be sick, thought Virgillia with alarm. Just like a picture flashed on a screen disappears from view, that is how thoughts of her promotion to Donald Long's office vanished from Virgillia's mind after she heard of Giuseppe's unexpected illness.

"Ma said he has a bellyache. Maybe, she said, he drank an extra glass of wine on an empty stomach," continued Caterina sitting again on the stoop, finding the place where she had left off in her fairytale.

Virgillia sighed with relief. A stomachache wasn't too bad, as long as it wasn't appendicitis. If ma wasn't alarmed his condition could not be too serious, she thought. She handed Caterina and Angie each a nickel and told them to buy an ice-cream cone after supper.

Silence reigned in the Vina flat when Virgillia entered. Maria wasn't singing her Italian ditties. She was annoyed because her daily routine had been disturbed. Giuseppe had come home from the shoe shine parlor moaning and groaning with a pain in his stomach.

"Ma, is Giuseppe very sick?" asked Virgillia as she drew the window shade and undressed. At that moment she pictured Donald's intent blue eyes as he drew the green shade protecting her from the sun's glare in the office. She felt a warm surge within herself.

"Rosalia thinks she knows everything when nothing happens. Then when something does happen she knows nothing. Giuseppe got a little bellyache and she runs for the doctor. Why doesn't she come to me asking, 'Ma, maybe we'll try a little fennel tea, or some camomile flowers in a bit of boiling water.' Even mint tea is a good for gas on the stomach." Maria seemed confounded as she spoke of Rosalia's helplessness in the midst of her own family trouble.

"Ma, doctors have to eat too, you know," soothed Virgillia.

"In Italy, those living in the country knew what herb to pick in the fields and for what ailment to use them. In America the doctor must tell you with a prescription what medicine to take because only he knows the secret." Virgillia laughed. She was accustomed to her mother's comparison of Italian customs versus the American way of life.

"Ma, we live in the greatest city in the world. Do you want to travel four hours to the mountains to pick a few herbs to cure Giuseppe's stomach? Wouldn't that be more expensive than calling a doctor?"

Maria smiled, nodding placidly. "Virgillia, you are a smart girl sometimes. I just don't make sense, always comparing Italy to America. New York City is the greatest city in the world, Virgillia, but sometimes I get homesick for the land and the customs to which I was born."

"You're right, ma. Rosalia could have used some home remedies before she called the doctor," Virgillia said, feeling empathy for her mother for feeling homesick.

"I'll still use fennel tea," announced Maria, "when I have gas on the stomach. Let Giuseppe drink that milky, chalky stuff called Milk of Magnesia."

"Where is Rosalia?" Virgillia gave the shade a slight tug and it flew up around the roller.

"Rosalia has been running up and down all day. She's scorching Guiseppe with hot towels on his stomach and freezing him with an ice bag on his head while dosing him with magnesia. She just left a while ago for the shoe shine parlor because she can't afford to lose customers."

Virgillia smiled. Giuseppe's problem should keep Rosalia out of my business for a while, she thought without malice.

"Hasn't Bettina come home yet? Where is Tommy? I never saw so many soiled dishes in the sink," exclaimed Virgillia desparingly.

"Tommy is doing homework in the front room. You know, Virgie, when Tommy sees dirty dishes in the sink, she never finishes her homework. I must talk to Father Ignatius about Tommy."

Maria moved heavily toward a chair, sat down, folded her arms on her chest and swayed sadly from side to side. "Sunday school doesn't seem to do much for Tommy," she lamented.

"You can only do what you understand, ma. I'll make Tommy understand her duties right this minute. I'll make religion sprout in her like a sunflower."

"Tommy," called Virgillia loudly. Tommy did not answer. Virgillia scraped the dishes, wiped her hands on her apron and went to the parlor in search of Tommy.

"Some people have ears and hear not," Maria quoted sadly.

Virgillia found Tommy seated before the open parlor window writing furiously. Her small figure was almost bent in two. Her feet rested on the chair rung bringing her knees to the level of a writing table.

"Tommy, did you hear me call?" Tommy paid no attention, as she accelerated her writing speed, her tongue lumping circles inside her cheek.

"Tommy! Did you hear me call?" Virgillia stamped her foot, exasperated. Tommy appeared oblivious of her surroundings, but her color was high and as bright as the red checkered dress she wore.

Virgillia tweaked her ear and Tommy looked up with a feigned, bewildered expression on her square face. Her long stiff bangs had loosened from their clips and hung over her small, bright eyes.

"I didn't hear you, I didn't hear you Virgie," she whined. Ma was right, thought Virgillia, some people had ears and didn't hear as the Good Book said.

"Does it take all afternoon to do a little homework. I never knew you liked homework that much, Tommy. You just hate to wash dishes and this is the easy way out," scolded Virgillia.

"Honest, Virgie, I don't like to do homework, but a girl copied from my test paper and teacher gave me extra homework." Disturbance lined Tommy's narrow forehead. "I'll soon be finished Virgie. I had to write I'll never cheat again one hundred times. You know how crazy some teachers can get, Virgie."

Virgillia bent over Tommy's shoulder. She looked closer. Tommy held her copy book more firmly as she felt Virgillia's close scrutiny. Virgillia waited for Tommy to finish writing, then she snatched the book from her.

"No, Tommy, I don't know how crazy a teacher can get but I know what a cheat Tommy can be." Virgillia turned the leaves of the notebook and took out one, two, three black carbon sheets.

"Is this how you do your homework? You're cheating everytime you're writing that you will never cheat again. Oh, Tommy!" Virgillia held the carbons and the notebook high above her head. Tommy stamped her feet tugging at her arm.

"Virgie, Virgie, Virgie," she pleaded, tears streaming down her cheeks. "Give me the book, please give it to me."

Virgillia tore the carbon sheets and the pages in the notebook on which she had written. Virgillia handed her the notebook with the original page on which she had written the sentence ten times.

"Wash the dishes this instant. Later, when I go downstairs to help Rosalia with the children, you may come with me and finish writing, 'I'll never cheat again,' where I can watch you." Tommy slowly walked to the kitchen, tears streaming down her cheeks.

Maria had been listening to the commotion in the parlor.

"Tommy, don't you know right from wrong? Isn't it easier to do what is right?" asked Maria, pitying the little scapegrace.

Tommy lifted her sudsy hands out of the dishpan and wiped her tears and running nose with her arm.

"Oh, ma, I know what's right but it's so much easier to do what's wrong," Tommy sobbed aloud as she washed the dishes.

"Sure it's easier to play bat and ball than it is to study, Tommy. If you want to be stupid in school then you must be willing to be a dunce, but be an honest dunce. Don't cheat and make yourself think you are being smart by outsmarting your teacher."

"Oh, shut up, Virgie." Tommy banged her feet on the floor and screeched.

Maria shook her finger back and forth at Virgillia to stop lecturing, then settled back in her chair and took her crocheting out of the cardboard box at her feet.

"Bettina will be home at ten o'clock tonight, Virgillia," informed Maria now that the problem of the dish washing was settled.

"Ten o'clock, ma? Why is she coming home so late?" asked Virgillia as she tucked her 'working clothes,' as the children called her better dresses, under the curtained recess in the second bedroom, returning hastily to the kitchen.

"Povera figlia. Bettina is such a good girl and she gets the hard knocks. Sometimes I think it is the evil eye of our neighbor, Signora Derella."

"How could Signore Derella give Bettina the evil eye when Bettina is going to marry her son, Roberto?" questioned Virgillia.

"Only Signore Derella believes in the evil eye, and she says only she can give it or take it away," ma said helplessly.

"Nonsense," said Virgillia impatiently.

"The boss at the five and ten cents store said that some of the morning help must work from two to ten o'clock at night and he picks on my Bettina," continued Maria.

"They work in shifts, ma. If Bettina works one or two weeks on the evening shift, after that she will return to day work for one or two weeks," explained Virgillia.

"But will Signore Derella believe that?" Maria turned anxious eyes on Virgillia who was folding the unpressed clothes on the old sewing machine.

Signora Derella was the thorn in the side of the Vinas. She lived in the flat on the left side of the hall. Since her husband passed away, the year before, she had taken to witchcraft. Ma and pa said she had gone soft in the head after she lost her tall, blonde husband. Perhaps, Virgillia often thought, ma and pa made excuses for her because her tall, dark and handsome son had fallen in love with Bettina. He was willing to wait for Bettina to mature and for Virgillia to find herself a husband before he married Bettina. Taking this into account, the Vinas who thought and spoke bluntly had to use every means at their disposal to treat Signora delicately, like a piece of rare bric a brac. After all, Roberto was good husband material, the Vinas reasoned.

"Why shouldn't Signora Derella believe Bettina?" asked Virgillia, but even as she asked she knew that Signora Derella believed only what she desired to believe and she was always telling ma pointedly that Roberto would never marry a girl like Virgillia who stayed out late at night. She even inferred sometimes that that was the reason Virgillia had not yet interested a fellow who would marry her because she stayed out late at night with Greta and flirted with men on the street.

"You know, Virgillia, how it is with some people. They don't want to believe what is true. They only want to believe what their minds make up," said Maria despairingly. Tommy's sobs subsided as she washed the dishes. Virgillia smiled gently. Tommy was simply a big baby with all her grown-up airs. Now Virgillia had a few minutes in which to dust the parlor.

The Vina parlor always seemed musty. The children left vestiges of their sooty, restless hands and feet everywhere. The green, cracked walls stood out in relief. The dying sun rays were harshly unflattering to the square old-fashioned room, with its secondhand, five-piece parlor set, which Rosalia had bought after she had married Giuseppe. She insisted that a well-furnished parlor would help her sisters to marry, as the furnishings would show a good background. Virgillia hated its muddy upholstery. She hated its old-fashioned curves and spiked ornaments that edged the top of the backs of the chairs. She had once seen a priceless five-piece set in an antique shop that had sent a sharp jab of joy through her. Its beauty had left her breathless. She could have these chairs painted a dull gold and have them covered with pastel shades of green or blue. Perhaps she would cover one with creamy satin. She smiled. Virgillia always smiled at her own absurdities. The fading sun rays shone in her eyes and suddenly she felt a warmth within her as she again remembered Donald as he lowered the green shade, his eyes intently watching her.

"Virgie, Virgie!" Virgillia arose with a start.

"Come and hear what Signore Derella is saying." Maria, Signora Derella, and Rosalia with Nicky and Nanny on her knees had formed a semicircle in the room. Virgillia came to the kitchen and carefully swept the papers with which the children had littered the floor, looking every now and then at Signora Derella to prove her interest. Signora Derella motioned

Maria and Rosalia to send the children to the parlor.

"They won't understand our conversation, besides they'll only use more gas light if they go into the parlor." Rosalia motioned with her hand to let the children stay where they were.

The Vinas disliked Signora Derella's interest in their family problems because she always wanted to work her foolish black magic on them. Now that she had heard Giuseppe had a stomachache, with her distorted mind, she thought she could wish it away, thought Virgillia. Signora Derella liked to feel the strength of her strange power with the occult over her audience, and for Bettina's sake, the Vinas played along with her. Signora Derella smoothed her straight black hair, which was coiled in a tight bun on the top of her head, as she slowly spoke, scanning each face with her beady black eyes.

"As soon as I heard Giuseppe was sick I knew I had to help him," she said solicitiously. "He is such a good, quiet man, and the father of three children. Povero, Giuseppe." She wrung her hands to match the sorrow on her thin face.

"Listen to me, Rosalia," she said confidently, "buy a little rabbit. Put him in a box on the fire escape for one week with no food. Remeber, no food." Signora Derella pointed a finger at Rosalia.

"Won't the rabbit die?" asked Rosalia.

"Don't ask any questions, Rosalia."

"I can't put the rabbit on my fire escape with all these children around. If they don't fall through the fire escape playing with the rabbit, they'll shove the rabbit down into the street. Do you understand, Signora Derella, why I can't put the rabbit on my fire escape?" Rosalia tried to keep a straight face, while Virgillia blew her nose to smother a laugh. Maria frowned at her daughters. It wouldn't do for Signora Derella to notice that she was being ridiculed. Maria put her crocheting in the cardboard box and fingered the rosary beads in the large pocket of her blue-and-white striped apron.

"I'll keep the rabbit on my fire escape," agreed Signora Derella. Maria now took the rosary beads from her pocket.

"Maria put those beads away. I can't think when I see them," Signora Derella said petulantly. Maria obediently put them in her pocket.

"Giuseppe can't stay home a whole week. He must go to the shoe shine parlor to work," said Rosalia.

"Eempa!" Signora Derella waved her hand in the air. "Guiseppe can go to work tomorrow. If you get the rabbit to-night you can cut some of the hairs, put them in a hot water bag, put the bag on his stomach, and the pains will stop for one week."

Caterina had finished her school homework. Now she and Angie were studying their catechism.

"I am the Lord, Thy God, thou shalt not have strange Gods before me." Over and over the children droned the first commandment.

Virgillia sat on the uncarpeted floor before the washtubs. Underneath the two tubs behind the ruffled blue gingham curtain the Vinas kept their pots and pans. Virgillia was putting them in order. If Signora Derella would only listen to Caterina and Angie at this moment would she understand that believing in the occult was a strange God, that being superstitious proved your belief in a power other than God? It was true as ma often quoted, "People have ears and hear not," thought Virgillia.

The door opened and Francesco came home for supper.

"Dio mio, it's six-thirty. Virgie set the table for supper." Maria slowly arose and walked with mincing steps to the door.

"Pa must be very hungry," said Maria as she poured olive oil over the cooked white beans in the saucepan. The sausages and potatoes were well browned and the prepared salad was in the icebox.

51

Rosalia, Maria, and Signora Derella each tried to tell Francesco about Giuseppe's bellyache, but when Signora Derella told him about her witchcraft, he winked at Maria and Rosalia and said, "You're right, Signora Derella, Rosalia must keep the rabbit on her fire escape because it is her husband who is being cured."

"A wise mouth speaks, Franci." Signora Derella laughed, a high cackling laugh, nodding her head vehemently in approval.

Nicky and Nanny had fallen asleep on Rosalia's lap. Rosalia, frowning, glanced at pa. She couldn't understand pa at times. Just when she had convinced Signora Derella to keep the rabbit on her fire escape, pa gave her the trouble of caring for it. Sometimes he just did not realize how much work she had to do, caring for her own family and helping ma. Now she had to worry about the rabbit. Caterina and Angie picked up their books and helped Virgillia set the table. After the table was set, Virgillia went into the parlor to see what Tommy was doing. She found her fast asleep, over her notebook where she had written for the hundredth time, "I'll never cheat again." Virgillia wondered at Tommy's kink in nature. Would she really never cheat again? We all have a kink in our nature, Virgillia thought reasonably. Signora Derella's kink was that she believed more in the powers of darkness than in the power of God. Rosalia was a busybody taking over everyone's life and work. Rosalia felt she was unselfish in helping ma. Unselfishness is a wonderful trait which makes martyrs and saints, thought Virgillia, but she hoped Rosalia would get off her back and not try to find her a husband.

"Tommy, Tommy. Supper is ready." Virgillia shook her gently, put her arm about her shoulders and led her to the kitchen.

Signora Derella had left, well satisfied that she had helped Giuseppe. Maria was glad that she had not asked for Bettina who had begun working on the evening shift in the five and ten cent store.

"Pa, why did you tell Signora Derella that I must put the rabbit on my fire escape when she agreed to take care of it?" questioned Rosalia, a trifle belligerent.

Pa laughed and winked mischievously at Maria's puzzled expression.

"Signora Derella has lost the way, Rosalia." Francesco pointed to his temple. "If she puts the rabbit on her fire escape you would have to buy a rabbit and you can't afford it right now. We'll put Piena, the cat Giuseppe has in the shoe shine parlor, in a box and feed him every day. When Signora Derella looks down from her window she'll think you have a rabbit in the box, but it will only be our cat."

Everyone laughed hilariously.

"What has the poor cat done to do such penance?" asked Maria as she brought the pot of beans to the table.

"To the good, God gives the grace to suffer for the bad who are too callous to ever come to terms with themselves. Every wrong act must be atoned for in the world, Maria mia," philosphized Francesco.

Maria nodded, "Yes, every sin against man and God must be expiated by man," agreed Maria who was deeply spiritual and God-fearing.

"Charity is a great virtue," giggled Rosalia, "and Piena will have to be charitable toward us in this instance and help us out of our dilemma."

Virgillia shrugged her shoulders. How could a human being know if Piena had the virtue of charity and if she did not, why force it on her, she thought as she poured the wine into the glasses on the table, hoping that Tom Mulvaney was not watching her from his kitchen window. She should have explained to him at the dance that her father squeezed grapes and made grape juice, which Italians drank with their meals, but that was not hard liquor, which she never drank.

When the sausages were served, Tommy took a bit off her sausage, put it in on a small dish and passed it around the table.

"Each of you give a bit of your sausage for Piena for there's no mice on the fire escape, and we don't want Piena to starve," said Tommy as she watched with calculating eyes on how much of the sausage each one was willing to offer.

"Remember, Tommy, the sausage is for Piena and not for you. No cheating," joked Virgillia.

Maria frowned at Virgillia and nodded approvingly at Tommy. Perhaps she wouldn't have to talk to Father Ignatius about Tommy's escapades after all. Piena was the only one who could bring out Tommy's kind, unselfish streak, thought Maria. Perhaps we don't understand her.

Tommy let Virgillia's cutting remark pass unnoticed. Now she was busily thinking of the fun she was going to have feeding trapped Piena on the fire escape, and it was going to be even more fun keeping Signora Derella away from Rosalia's fire escape. Suddenly Tommy laughed aloud as she imagined the expression of consternation on Signora Derella's face if she should discover that the rabbit was Piena the cat. No one questioned Tommy's sudden burst of laughter because just then Giuseppe entered. Nicky and Nanny were sleeping on Maria's brass bed. Rosalia had been invited for supper. Giuseppe looked pale but said the Milk of Magnesia had worked wonders. Maria quickly prepared her favorite egg soup for Giuseppe. This was her contribution to convalescent stomachs. She cut several sprigs of parsely in boiling water, added two beaten eggs, a drop of olive oil, and poured the egg soup in a large bowl. She served it with bread croutons made from toasted bread cut in tiny squares.

While Giuseppe ate the soup he heard of the plans to fool Signora Derella with her witchcraft. He doubled up with laughter. He said the gas pains were all gone but it would be just as well to go along with Signora Derella and make her think she had cured him so she would feel warmer toward Bettina, her future daughter in law.

Francesco took one of the boards that made up the girls' bed, sawed it, and make a box for Piena, drilling holes in it for air. When Maria remonstrated that he was using the bed board, he said there were still enough boards to hold up the mattress.

"There!" he exclaimed contentedly after he finished his work. "No one will know if there is a cat or a rabbit in the box." Just then Bettina came home from the five and ten cents store.

"Did you meet Signora Derella?" asked Maria anxiously.

"I'll try not to let her see me, ma. She isn't well and I don't want to upset her with her silly thoughts that that I run around by myself in the evening," said Bettina kindly.

"Good girl, Bettina," Francesco patted her shoulder.

After Bettina heard of how they were going to let Signora Derella believe that she was curing Giuseppe with her witchcraft, Bettina said, "When Signora Derella gets well, I will tell her about Piena the cat. She will laugh too."

Maria gazed at the Madonna. God knows what He is doing, Madonna Mia. He is giving Bettina a good husband and Signora Derella a fine daughter and above all He is giving Bettina the grace to understand Signora Derella, thought Maria gratefully.

SIX

Virgillia was surprised to find Mr. Long at his desk the following morning. She was a bit nettled to see her work of the previous day in disorder on her desk. The filing cabinets were open and the records in disarray. Half a dozen of them were open on Donald's desk. He looked up with a bright smile, his brow a bit furrowed.

"Good Morning, Miss Vina. Get busy. We're moving." He drew up his leg which he had flung in the aisle between the two desks. Virgillia looked with surprise at the fine crease of his gray trouser as she came down the cleared passage to her seat beside him. Slowly she took off her hat and gloves as she questioned, "We're moving?"

"The firm is opening a branch office uptown."

Her heart gave a thud leaving her breathless. Would she go along with him or would she remain in the present office.

"Please get me the folder for Fairchild, Inc., there are a dozen Fairchilds in the files and I can't seem to locate the right one."

"You want the Fairchild with the George in it. He wants the English Tudor type house."

"I'm doing good. New office, new efficient secretary," said Donald. Virgillia took a deep breath. She felt like shouting hurrah like Tommy did when in a merry mood. She was going with him, with Mr. Donald Long. Looking at her, he wondered why Virgillia, for no apparent reason, smiled to herself. Deftly she adjusted a loose ringlet of black hair, dabbed a puff to her nose. The cream-colored jabot became unfastened at her throat, baring her soft, firm flesh above her breast. She wiped her glasses, which she only wore for the office, on the cotton lace jabot. Donald handed her his white, linen handkerchief. For a moment she didn't understand his gesture, then swift realization brought the color rushing to her cheeks as she fastened the jabot.

"I got that terrible habit from associating with women. The girls in the stenographic department never look for handkerchiefs during busy hours," she apologized. He laughed, their feeling of strangeness melting. As she bent over the filing cabinet, Donald noted the molded suppleness of her slim, young body. He had never noticed Margaret's plump figure. The faint morning sunlight shone on the curve of her cheeks and slightly upturned, deeply cleft chin.

"I'm glad we're moving," Virgillia said, placing the correct folder before Mr. Long.

"Why?" he asked curiously meeting her glance.

She was filing numerically some papers in her hand.

"I'll have a chance to explore the upper part of Manhattan during lunch hour. Enough of Wall Street."

"Funny girl," he thought, and then because since time immemorial man has been the hunter, the plan for a chase took root.

"Our office is moving this afternoon. How about doing a bit of exploring together?" Astonishment took Virgillia's breath away.

He arose, his hands sunk in his pockets. She looked at him speechless. The sun shone on his smooth, black hair. Her hesitancy piqued him. Margaret had never hesitated to go with him anywhere. Why was she hesitating? Unconsciously he fisted his hands in his pockets.

"Won't you like to explore the upper part of New York with me?" he questioned, an uncertain smile hovering over his parted lips.

If she could only control her heartbeats. She had been to

many dances with Greta, but she had never met anyone like Donald Long.

"Yes," she said breathlessly. "I would like it very much."

Donald unclenched his hands. He felt like a frozen stream thawing with the heat of a summer sun.

Donald now gave his work all his attention, to make up for the half-day lapse while the office moved uptown. Virgillia kept steady pace with his demands. She gathered the unwanted folders, replaced them in the files and filled his chromium pitcher with the large knobbed cover with cool water from the spring water bottle in the corner. Reaching for a pencil from the group that Virgillia had sharpened and placed in his pencil tray, his fingers touched the cool perspiring pitcher. He looked surprised.

"I have never used this pitcher," he said.

"From now on, you will use it," she answered quietly. He almost felt rebuked for not having used it before. Another time he found her looking at him critically.

"You can't be comfortable in that position, Mr. Long. Your shoulders slouch." Reared in her large family at home, it was natural for the Vinas to be concerned about each other and solicitous of human beings in general with whom they came in contact. Now that she was working for Mr. Long, Virgillia took a personal interest in his welfare in the office. Obediently he shortened his swivel chair bringing his arms to the level of his desk and realized that his shoulders felt more rested after a few hours work.

But during lunch and on their ride uptown, it was Donald who took the lead, choosing one of the better restaurants and later taking the Fifth Avenue bus to Riverside Drive. It had been years since he had sat in one of the open air seats atop a Fifth Avenue bus and gone for a joy ride. It was early spring, the air was cool and crisp, and the sun shone brightly. For Virgillia, it was an especially brilliant sunlight that sparked everything she saw, dipping it in gold, as she sat relaxed with Donald by her side. The brim of her navy blue felt hat was turned up at one side, her trim navy blue coat buttoned to her throat. Her white gloved hands were loosely clasped on her lap. John's blue eyes kept pace with Virgillia's chatter as she remarked about the bustling crowds and the New York skyline, which like the city itself is forever changing. He felt a stranger in his own city, as if he and Virgillia were seeing it for the first time.

"Everyone, everything is moving," said Virgillia watching the people hurrying and scurrying this way and that, jostling each other, noting the quick fleeting smiles of apology of the jostlers entirely lost on the people hustling in the opposite direction.

They passed the shopping district. Virgillia had taken off her gloves. Now she caught Donald's hand.

"Look at that beautiful window display, Donald." It was the first time she had called him Donald. They looked at each other and laughed like two children.

"It is fascinating, Virgillia," he said, leaning slightly forward toward the rail of the bus, his face coming close to her own. One of the department stores had created a village. Mannequins dressed in native style from countries all over the world stood or sat at ease behind the huge store window.

"That display is typical of New York," said Donald thoughtfully, "millions of different races, rooted, merged, expanding. It is like the splendor of the ages giving the grace of youth to a country steeped in freedom. This is New York—America." Virgillia felt his mood. She wished she could take ma, pa, and Rosalia on a bus trip to see the window display. She knew how impossible was her wish. Ma, pa, and Rosalia were rooted in their niches and were happy in them. The world with its displays and achievements did not interest ma, pa and Rosalia, as much as finding husbands for the daughters as they came of age.

"Don't you think American woman are the most beautiful, Donald?" She was unprepared for his answer.

"I think you are the most beautiful girl I have ever met." Virgillia flushed at the compliment and even though he pressed the fingers of her hand, he seemed to be looking at her in a detached way, as though he was comparing her with some other girl he knew. Donald was comparing Virgillia. He was comparing her with Margaret. How were they alike and how did they differ? Margaret was an architect like himself. He and Margaret had the common interest of their careers. In coloring Margaret was blonde with large blue eyes. Virgillia was brunette. Personality wise Virgillia was bright and gay. Margaret was moody. The moment passed. Donald and Virgillia laughed at a man on stilts who winked at them as he passed with a huge sign on his back advertising men's clothes. The bus stopped with a jolt throwing Donald and Virgillia together. A stab of pleasurable pain coursed through their bodies. Passengers were getting on the bus. The New York public library between Forty and Forty-second Street stood before them.

"A little over a century ago there was potter's field where the library now stands. After they removed the cemetery, a reservoir was built on the property, then in 1853 the Crystal Palace was erected."

"Did you make a special study of this particular corner?" teased Virgillia, amazed at his fund of knowledge.

"I'll never forget this corner of New York City. When I was editor of the college paper, I was assigned to write a piece on it. It wasn't easy to gather the information, and I never forgot it."

"What else happened on this corner?" asked Virgillia, her eyes brimming with laughter.

"Let me see if I remember." Donald crinkled his eyes. "The Crystal Palace burned, the reservoir was torn down at the turn of the century, and the Tilden, Astor, and Lenox libraries were consolidated into the present library."

"You sound like a guide on a tour, Donald."

"The public library took twenty years to complete. Do you see the figures above the entrance?" Virgillia like other people rushing here and there had never stopped to notice the figures.

"They are beautiful," admitted Virgillia.

"They depict history, drama, poetry, religion, romance, and philosphy." Donald genuinely enjoyed his roll of schoolboy reciting a lesson.

"Anything else happened on this corner?" asked Virgillia curiously. She wished this ride would never end.

"You and I took a ride on a bus," grinned Donald, "and the bus stopped on this corner." He pressed her hand gently.

Virgillia now looked at the tall buildings as the bus sped by.

"Most modern structures today are flat," she said.

"The beauty of modern architecture today is the lack of beauty." Virgillia pondered the thought. Donald was right.

She saw the spires of Saint Patrick's Cathedral. Vaguely she wondered, if she tried to grasp this adventure as an avenue opening into a new life, would it evade her as the tall gothic spires of the cathedral that appeared on a level with the top of the bus, only to shoot in the air as they neared the church. A wedding was in progress. She glimpsed an ermine wrapped bride walking up the red carpeted steps. Strains of Lohengrin's wedding march floated across the wind.

"How beautiful!" she murmured. To Virgillia, riding carefree on top of the bus with Donald beside her, away from the Vina flat, life at its rosiest loomed before her. Accepting Donald's invitation had been a challenge to Virgillia. A challenge against her good, Italian immigrant parents who wanted to control her heart and mind and have her live the kind of life they thought would be best for her, rather than have her discover for herself what would be best for her. A challenge against Luigi and Salvatore who might bring her an unwanted

61

suitor. She sighed. Donald turned toward her.

"Tired?" he asked solicitiously.

"No," she sighed again. "It has been wonderful, but I must be home at the usual time." He did not question her.

"We'll have supper first?" he asked almost hopefully. It would be better than dining alone with the maid serving him, he thought dismally.

Virgillia thought of pa and ma glancing at the clock if she were too late for supper. No, she didn't want them to worry more than they took it upon themselves to worry about her, neither did she care to make explanations.

"No, Donald. Thank you," she answered softly.

"We can have something to drink then. I am thirsty and you prescribed drinking for me, Virgillia." His eyes twinkled.

"I'll have a coke," she agreed.

He had been kind, this strange, new personality who had come suddenly into her life. Virgillia recalled his features as she returned home, his flat chin with its hint of firmness, the unusual wide forehead, sharpening the contours of his firm, lean jaw. Thoughts of him submerged all seeming important matters to mere trivialities, lending wings to her feet and a song to her heart.

And Donald walking through the dusky paths of Central Park wrestled with his emotions. Her well modulated voice kept ringing in his ears, "What else happened on this corner." He had wanted to crush her in his arms and smother her with kisses saying and this also happened on the corner of Forty-second Street and Fifth Avenue, but no, he had to bide his time. He had to make sure that Virgillia returned his love. Now he questioned himself without reserve. Had he been in love with Margaret or had he been in love with his ambition of seeing their names over their office, Long and Long, Architects. Slowly, thoughtfully, Donald wended his way homeward.

SEVEN

Opposite the tenement that housed the Vinas, an old two-story house had been converted into a Jewish synogogue. Virgillia coming home from the office on Saturday afternoon saw a not uncommon sight on the East Side in the early twenties, where Jews, newly landed in New York City from all over the world, practiced their foreign customs as did all immigrants who settled in the melting pot of Manhattan.

A funeral was in progress. A rabbi was murmuring the last rites over a coffin in the street. Virgillia stopped to watch. She always waited for the hearse to shut its doors on the coffin. The mourners then would crowd around the closed doors, beating their fists and sobbing unrestrainedly for the dear, departed one. Virgillia felt sorry for the mourners who could not resolve their loss. They would follow the hearse on foot crying loudly and wringing their hands. Their cries and beating fists now came between Virgillia and her thoughts of Donald. Suddenly she felt aware of her surroundings as she breathed the stale smells of the garbage cans. The cries and beating fists seemed so futile, as futile as her own wish to meet and marry a man of her own choosing as against one introduced to her by her well-meaning family, spurred by Rosalia's feelings of responsibility toward her younger sisters. Would the man with whom she fell in love be in love with her? Would Donald love her? A vision of the far flung spires of Saint Patrick's Cathedral came before her. She tried to recapture the vision of herself and Donald riding carefree atop the Fifth Avenue bus. Donald seemed merged with the distant spires of the cathedral.

Climbing the stairs of the old tenement, she heard frantic

yells coming from Rosalia's apartment. She stood still and listened. Virgillia grasped the shaky bannister to steady herself. Had Giuseppe become ill again? Perhaps he died. She took a deep breath then opened the kitchen door. Her momentary fright had been so great that now as she watched the children she didn't know whether to laugh or cry for sheer relief.

Tommy stood in the middle of the kitchen floor tearing her wiry, straw colored hair, beating her fists in the air, distorting her large mouth in ugly shapes as she imitated the mourners in their grief. Nicky imitated Tommy, shrieking at the top of his voice while Nanny held a huge turkish towel to her eyes, her shoulders heaving up and down as though she was sobbing.

Seated on the floor, Caterina and Angie were struggling with Piena. The cat had been in the box all week and was now trying to regain his freedom.

"Hold on to the corpse," shouted Tommy, "cause we can't have a funeral without a corpse."

"Hurry with the funeral will you? Piena doesn't want to stay," gasped Caterina. Virgillia bent over the children and gently stroked the cat.

Rosalia changing the bed linens peered though the doorway. "Virgillia, Giuseppe needs the cat in the shoe shine parlor. The mice are all over the place, but Signora Derella told ma that if a week didn't starve the rabbit, maybe two weeks would do it. What shall I do, Virgillia?" Virgillia smiled to herself. For once Rosalia seemed to be at a loss for a solution. Virgillia had read somewhere that it was the little things that made up life. Did they have to be foolish things like Signora Derella and the rabbit and Rosalia who instead of starving a rabbit had fattened a cat? Suddenly she felt irritable. Her morning in the new office had been disappointing. Donald had been detained in the downtown office. At the new address he would preside in a modern styled office, behind a door marked *PRIVATE*. She would be in a small adjoining room with her typewriter, filing cabinets and a buzzer.

"Must the children yell so loudly Rosalia?" she questioned almost angrily.

"Let them have fun, Virgillia. They were watching the funeral across the street, and all of a sudden Tommy thought of having a funeral because Signora Derella expected the rabbit to die today."

"I don't think the playing is funny," said Virgillia.

"Look, look, Virgie. Watch Nicky and Nanny. Aren't they cute, the way they make believe sobbing?"

A knock sounded on the kitchen door. Tommy had made good progress with the funeral. The children walked around and around the room screeching and yelling while Caterina and Angie wrestled with the huge, fatted cat. Virgillia turned hesitatingly to Rosalia.

"It's Signora Derella," she said in a loud whisper.

Caterina and Angie instantly let go of the cat who ran out of the kitchen window.

"Quick children, run downstairs and chase the cat to Giuseppe's store." Rosalia shooed the children out the door, as she smiled ingratiatingly at Signora Derella, then her face changed to a mournful expression.

"I have bad news, Signora Derella. The animal in the box didn't die. It just ran out the window." Contrary to her expectations Signora Derella laughed in high glee, slapping Rosalia on the shoulder.

"That is good news, Rosalia. The rabbit ran away? That means Giuseppe will live a long life and his pains will go and never return. It's just like a miracle, a miracle!" chanted Signora Derella, then suddenly her eyes narrowed and she stared searchingly at Rosalia.

"Only one thing you must learn, Rosalia. You must never call a rabbit an animal. The rabbit will get insulted. Yes, ma'am, and you will undo the charm." Signora Derella fiercely shook her finger under Rosalia's nose. Virgillia and Rosalia exchanged fleeting smiles.

"Remember, Rosalia, a rabbit must be called a rabbit," finished Signora Derella, well pleased with her witchcraft.

Later that afternoon Rosalia and Virgillia related the incident of Signora Derella's predictions and how the cat ran away, while she thought it was the rabbit who took flight. The assembled family laughed but Maria was thoughtful.

"Is it right to allow a deluded soul to believe she is doing right believing in witchcraft?" she asked slowly. Maria's simple faith was strong within her. During long winter evenings she related Bible stories to her children before the red, hot kitchen stove. The stove softened the hardest chestnuts and as the children munched the treat, Maria with simple words drew pictures of the ancient prophets who spoke of God. It irked Maria at times that the family went along with Signora Derella's faith in witchcraft.

"Ma, do you want her to interfere in Roberto's love for Bettina?" Rosalia would ask, her buck teeth shining belligerently. Francesco looked thoughtful as he glanced at the straightforward eyes of the Madonna looking at him.

"Rosalia, ma is right. If Signora Derella could be taught to think right, Bettina will have an easier life with her as a mother-in-law, after she marries Roberto," he said.

"But Signora Derella thinks she is thinking right," said Giuseppe tolerantly.

"She thinks she is right because she has set herself up as a martyr. After her husband died, if she had prayed, 'Thy will be done, dear Father, on earth as it is in heaven,' " Maria piously crossed herself, "she would have accepted her husband's trip to heaven and she wouldn't have gone half out of her mind, angry because her husband passed away."

"Perhaps she made a mistake and prayed, 'My will be done, dear Father, on earth, not as it is in heaven,' " said Rosalia laughing while Virgillia giggled.

Giuseppe hunched his shoulders and spread out his palms helplessly.

"All I know is that she spoiled my cat. Piena was a good mouser before we gave him a vacation in the box on the fire escape plus plenty of food. This afternoon all he did was sit before the store window and purr himself to sleep in the sunshine." Giuseppe paused bewildered, then added, "He even was too lazy to wash his face today. The mice ran all round him and he looked away disdainfully."

"The sausage meat tastes better," giggled Tommy. "Tonight I'll pass the dish for him again."

"Oh, no you won't, Tommy," exclaimed Virgillia. "Piena's vacation is over. You're not going to make a panhandler out of him."

"He'll have to return to work in the store if he wants to eat," stated Giuseppe firmly.

Through with their late lunch, Virgillia began the Saturday afternoon housecleaning. Roberto was playing with Rollo on the sofa. Virgillia knew he was allowing the baby to gnaw his finger with his toothless gums to assuage his disappointment at not finding Bettina at home. On this particular afternoon, Virgillia missed Bettina too, because she had promised to see the operetta *Glass Shutters* with Greta. Bettina always helped her with the Saturday housecleaning. She was anxious to get through her work quickly this afternoon.

"Where is Bettina, Virgie?" Roberto was puzzled. "She hasn't been home any evening this week. Where is she now?"

Maria moved slowly towards the parlor, her fat fingers nimbly crocheting.

"Ma, Roberto wants to know where Bettina goes when she isn't at home," said Virgillia as she scurried around the room, shaking the sofa pillows out the window.

Maria made herself comfortable in a corner of the sofa.

"Mama mia, Roberto," she drawled amiably, "I can't find a moment's peace. Don't worry, Roberto, Bettina is at a safe place."

"I haven't seen my girl for a week," scowled Roberto, drawing himself to his full height.

"I wish Bettina were here too, Roberto. She always helps me clean the flat on Saturday afternoon. Ma, tonight I'm going to see an operetta with Greta. I must get through cleaning early."

"I don't worry so much, Virgillia, when you're in a theater with Greta, but when you go dancing with strange men, I keep praying that God keeps you safe," said Maria slowly.

"Signora Vina, why don't you worry about Bettina?" asked Roberto jealously.

"Oofa, Roberto," Maria waved her hand in the air. "Signora Derella is calling you. Go, go before she'll start worrying about you."

"Ma only calls me when she needs these." Roberto jingled the coin in his pocket. They laughed at the truth of his statement. Roberto whisked the dust cloth out of Virgillia's hand.

"I'll do Bettina's share of the cleaning," he looked shyly at Maria with his round, brown eyes.

"Ma, did Bettina go to Cousin Marietta?" asked Virgillia with a twinkle in her eyes. Roberto laughed aloud. Only Maria went to see spinster Cousin Marietta, in her spacious home in Flatbush, Brooklyn, at certain periods in her life. Most of the Vina children had been born there. She was an eccentric woman, past forty, who lived alone. She had been successful in the designing field and was financially independent. She had been present when one of Maria's children had been born in the crowded Vina flat and had offered, in a moment of pity and generosity, her home to be used for the births of future Vina children. It had lightened the burden for Maria and Francesco because Cousin Marietta even paid the bill for the midwife.

Roberto had grown up with the Vina girls, playing cops and robbers on the roof. He knew all their intimate family secrets.

"Virgillia, you know that only your mother goes to Cousin Marietta and you know the reason why," said Roberto.

Maria continued to crochet, smiling pleasantly to herself. Roberto was tall, dark and handsome. He was very kind too, not like his poor, deluded mother. Signora Derella's mind told her many things that were untrue. She must not be told that Bettina worked during the evenings, but Roberto had a right to know. He loved Bettina and was willing to wait until Virgillia married, if only Luigi and Salvatore would hurry and bring her a suitor. They had paid Giuseppe a visit in the shoe shine parlor yesterday and had again promised to pay the Vinas a visit just to meet Virgillia.

Roberto had cleaned the parlor quickly and well. Gently he placed Rollo on Maria's bed, holding the milk bottle as the baby drained it. Virgillia felt suddenly sorry for his unfulfilled desire of not seeing Bettina for a whole week.

"Oh, ma, let's tell Roberto where Bettina goes during the evenings and where she is this afternoon."

"I was thinking of the same thing, Virgillia," admitted Maria. Roberto had passed the test for letter carrier. He would look handsome with the blue uniform and so impressive carrying the large, brown leather bag filled with letters, flung across his broad shoulders. Yes, Roberto was a good catch, a very good catch for Bettina. God was good, thought Maria.

Maria put her crocheting on her lap and said in a loud whisper, afraid her voice would carry to Signora Derella's open window, "Bettina's hours at the five and ten cent store have been changed Roberto. For a while she must work from two to ten o'clock in the evening. We don't want your mother to know because she might fabricate stories about Bettina being out evenings and turn you against her."

Roberto nodded in agreement and sighed with relief.

Roberto knew his mother magnified trifling incidents. She had changed after his father's death. He loved Bettina dearly for herself and he loved her more because she was kind and considerate of his sick mother.

"Tell Bettina I'll take her to the twelve o'clock mass tomorrow, Signora Vina," he said happily. Then turning to Virgillia, he added, "Virgillia, I'll give you a year to fall in love because I'm marrying Bettina two years from now.'

"Fair enough," smiled Virgillia, "but you have my permission to marry her tomorrow."

"Don't talk like that, Virgillia." Maria shook her head reprovingly. "If your younger sister marries before you, everyone will point a finger at you and wonder why no young man wanted you and you'll remain an old maid."

"Ma, you speak ridiculously sometimes," shrugged Virgillia.

While Virgillia dressed herself to meet Greta, Maria prepared for la spesa. She and Rosalia would slowly promenade along the market section of Orchard Street, on the lower east side of Manhattan, where pushcart peddlars sold their wares, lined along the curbs. Rosalia sewed her own shopping bags made of oilcloth. Homemade bags were stronger and larger than those on sale. Maria and Rosalia would stroll leisurely, munching sour pickles, the shopping bags dangling from their arms as they evaluated the food and articles on display.

"Ma, are you ready?" asked Rosalia entering the kitchen, then softly shutting the door, she said in a low tone, "Signora Derella asked me to buy her cow horns, ma. She wants pa to shine them up for her and put them on a stand."

"Doesn't Signora Derella have anything better to worry about?" asked Maria with annoyance. In Italy, superstitious people believe that cow horns took evil away.

Rosalia looked at Virgillia and giggled.

"She believes some one gave Virgillia the evil eye because

70

she says Virgillia is a beautiful girl, and she doesn't have a sweetheart as Bettina has, who is younger. She thinks the cow horns will take away the evil eye from Virgillia."

Virgillia was putting on her black turban. She held it in midair as she turned to look with exasperation at Rosalia.

"Signora Derella just finished working her magic on Giuseppe, she better not climb on my back," scolded Virgillia.

"Don't talk like that Virgillia. Signora Derella only wants to help you, even if it is a foolish way of helping, poor soul. She means well," said Maria quietly for she only wanted to see good in people. It was less stressful.

"I don't see why Bettina wants to live in the same house with her after she marries Roberto, ugh!" Virgillia hunched her shoulders as though she was running away from some gruesome monster.

"Virgie, God will be good to Bettina because she is kind." She looked sharply at Virgillia. "Must Roberto throw his old mother in the street? He is her only son."

"Virgillia lives in a dream world, ma. She thinks she will always be young and the handsome man she expects to marry will have no earthly attachments." Rosalia looked down her nose at her sister. Virgillia slipped into her short black coat.

"Rosalia, I may live in a dreamworld, but neither are you realistic. God doesn't always reward the good in this world," said Virgillia empathically. She was good, she thought, yet she was owned heart and mind by her own family, not only owned, but possessed.

"Life is give and take, Virgie. I brought you into the world, protected and loved you and when I get old, won't you take care of me, too, if I should need you?" Virgillia looked at her mother whose face puckered as though she was about to cry.

"Ma, you'll never get old like Signora Derella, you're much too busy and some of your children will always need you." Then impulsively she threw her arms about her mother and pressed her chin on her mother's fleshy shoulder. "You know ma, Rosalia won't let anyone else have you."

"I'm the oldest, ma. You'll never leave me and Giuseppe and the children. We will always need you, ma." Rosalia said with glowing pride.

EIGHT

Virgillia threaded her way along the dark streets lit by the fitful lights of the stores which were open until midnight on the lower east side of Manhattan during 1920. Dozens of children played games and danced folk dances on the crowded New York streets. Games and dances which they learned in school. Greta was waiting for her by the doorway of her tenement. Her straight blonde hair was parted and sleeked, rolled in a large bun at the nape of her neck. Her large, blue eyes sparkled in the midst of darkened, curly lashes.

"I'm sorry, Virgillia. Pete came home on an unexpected furlough. First one since he joined the army. He is taking me out," but added hastily, as she read disappointment in Virgillia's eyes, "he can get you a blind date, if you care to come along." Virgillia shook her head negatively. She would rather be alone, free to do as she pleased than spend an uncomfortable evening with a strange man she might not like.

Virgillia opened her bag to return the tickets to Greta.

"Pete doesn't care for that long hair stuff, Virgillia. You may keep the tickets." Virgillia's face brightened instantly.

"Oh, I don't mind going alone Greta. Thanks a million for the tickets."

"Aren't you taking anyone with you?" asked Greta.

"No. Have a nice evening with Pete."

"We'll manage," tittered Greta as she looked after Virgillia's trim, retreating figure.

"Funny girl, that one," she murmured.

To Virgillia, boarding a crosstown streetcar, riding uptown, away from the tenements, stale garbage smells and her family's plans to ensnare a husband for her, gave her a sense of freedom which lifted her spirits, but to see Donald standing before the theater was indeed a miracle to Virgillia. He was loitering before the gates of the playhouse. She stood before him, slim and tall. How glad she felt that she had dressed with unusual care. Her black silk turban with a penciled line of yellow threaded through the thick coiled band encircling it, ending with a huge knot above her parted, black hair, matched her black silk dress trimmed with yellow ruching, which rested against her throat. Her short black coat, which she had bought at a bargain price, at a special sale, had loose puffed sleeves, showing frilled yellow cuffs. She felt in line with the thousands of trim, business girls out for an evening's entertainment along Broadway, called the Great White Way, because of its millions of sparkling electric lights.

Donald regarded her with a happy smile. She was surprised that he seemed to expect her.

"It is indeed a pleasure for you to be on time. Women are usually late," he teased.

"I'm so glad you were going to wait for me," she countered, delighted to see him. "Are you going to see *Glass Shutters?*" Donald nodded. "I hope you haven't bought your ticket because I have two passes." Excitedly she searched through her handbag.

"What a coincidence to meet you here!" Her voice held a note of pleasurable surprise. How nice of him to make believe he was waiting for her and she was late, she thought, at the turn of affairs. Donald stood looking at her, slightly puzzled. He remembered seeing the two passes drop from her pocketbook, one morning, the week before they moved to their new office. He had purposely come this evening to see who would be Virgillia's escort. That was the reason why he refused Ben Worth's invitation to see *Glass Shutters* with Virgillia, as Ben had suggested. Why was she seeing the play alone when she had two passes, he questioned himself, but could find no adequate answer.

"This is my lucky evening." He took her arm with feigned gallantry.

"You were standing there as though you were waiting just for me," laughed Virgillia, amazed at her good fortune of meeting Donald and wishing it were true that Donald had been waiting for her.

Sitting beside Virgillia in the theater, holding her hand, brought him back to his teen years, when he left the farm to work his way through college. Taking a girl to the movies every now and then was his only recreation at the time. He spent two years in France, then after the First World War, he returned to work for his college degree. It had been difficult, an uphill battle. He finally achieved success and gained recognition as an architect when he met Margaret with whom he could discuss his work. He had felt grievously hurt when Margaret broke her engagement to him, to marry her boyhood friend, Doctor Blane. He felt grieved but never dreamed that in time, he would be attracted to a girl, the complete opposite of Margaret. Virgillia, a simple girl, who, with the eagerness of youth, would innocently lead him atop a Fifth Avenue bus and together find delight exploring the wonders of New York, wonders which New Yorkers see with unseeing eyes.

Now together they lived the despair and tragedy of *Glass Shutters*, the most exciting play on Broadway. Together they emerged smiling and happy at its joyous ending. Donald had never experienced such joy in depth with Margaret.

"Would that my heart lived within glass shutters," repeated Donald, murmuring the words of the musical covering Virgillia's hand which rested on the softly lighted table in one of the restaurants within the theater district.

The musical had had a fantastic twist. The heroine in love with two men thinks she has chosen the right one until waiting at the altar about to repeat the marriage vows, she glances at the best man who is her jilted suitor and realizes she has chosen the wrong lover. She makes a wish, "Would that my heart lived within glass shutters" and immediately every one of her wishes is magically made known. The jilted suitor realizes at once that the heroine loves him. The groom disappears, the curtain goes down on their marriage.

Donald felt glad that Virgillia had magically made him understand that he had not been in love with Margaret. He had been in love with Margaret's career, which was like his own. He had seen their names linked in their careers, LONG AND LONG, ARCHITECTS, in electric lights over the door of his own firm.

Virgillia smiled at Donald.

"What a beautiful fantasy," she said. She was unusually quiet after that. Donald looked up from the menu and saw Virgillia staring into space, looking perturbed. A sudden glimpse of her family and Signora Derella anxiously finding her a husband flashed through her mind, then catching Donald's eyes, she laughed.

"Your thoughts seem to be as disturbing as those of our heroine," he teased.

She flushed.

"Wouldn't you want me to know your thoughts?" he asked gently. She didn't answer his questions as she toyed with her fork. He wondered with a pang if he wasn't taking Virgillia too much for granted. He didn't know anything about her private life. Why did Virgillia come alone when she had two passes. Had she quarrelled with her boyfriend? The thoughts persisted, spoiling his evening.

"Donald, these are delicious. I've never eaten them before—like this." Donald stared at the shrimp cocktail set before him. Virgillia was picking at the shrimps daintily with her fork. At the sound of her voice he pushed his doubts away from him.

It was impossible that Virgillia had never eaten shrimps before.

"What do you mean you never ate shrimps like this?" asked Donald.

"I've eaten shrimps, fried in batter, in tomato sauce, but never in a tall stemmed flat glass like this." Everything seemed new and thrilling to Virgillia who rarely ate in restaurants. She would never tire of anything, thought Donald. Life would be forever new and young for her.

They finished their dinner. She found herself dancing, swaying rythmically back and forth, steered gently by Donald's strong arm. She felt as though she was wafting through space.

"You dance as beautiful as you look," he murmured. Suddenly Donald felt a tickle in his nose. He stopped dancing and frantically searched for his handkerchief. He found it in time to catch a sneeze. A tiny valentine card dropped at Virgillia's feet. She picked it up and couldn't help reading the bold, black letters.

"Darling Donald, I love you—Meg."

Virgillia felt strangely chilled in the warm restaurant.

"I'm sorry I spoiled our dance." Then he saw the Valentine card in Virgillia's hand. He lumped his tongue in his cheek.

"How did Saint Valentine come between us? He does love lovers," he quipped, slipping the card back in his breast pocket.

Virgillia looked deeply into Donald's eyes but all she could read was a deep tenderness. That look of tenderness, was it for Meg or for her? Everyone sent meaningless love notes on Saint Valentine's day, she tried to tell herself, but he did return the card to his breast pocket, over his heart, she thought.

After Virgillia left, Donald spent a restless night. The jangling streetcars and night noises did not disturb Virgillia's sleep. She was used to noisy nights but the little red Valentine card disturbed her. If they planned their rendezvous she would not have enjoyed it more. With Donald, dancing in his arms, she felt like the earth opening in the spring, bursting with new life. Who was Meg? Was she Donald's sweetheart? Why had he gone to the theater alone? Had he quarreled with Meg? She felt the hard boards underneath the mattress for the first time. Tommy's foot kicked her in the stomach.

"Stop moving, Virgie, will you?" Tommy withdrew her foot and turned on her pillow.

Virgillia sighed. She had accepted Donald's invitation to explore New York atop a Fifth Avenue bus as a lark. Her lark had turned to a song of love. The office gossips said that Donald was a confirmed bachelor who was only interested in his work. Donald was not a lady's man, they said. They probably didn't know the real Donald, thought Virgillia.

NINE

Virgillia had been aroused early and had gone to church with her mother and father. She had seen the sun rise over the sooty tenement roofs. Her heart returned the sun's warmth. Even news that Salvatore and Luigi were coming to dinner failed to band her heart with anxiety. Anxiety that they might find a suitor she would fall in love with, because she was already in love. Even if nobody knew it, even if Donald was unaware of her feelings, Virgillia knew that she was in love with Donald.

Coming home from church, Bettina and the children had been banished to Rosalia's apartment, as they usually were when the Vinas entertained consequential company. Giuseppe sat before the kitchen table with a pair of cow's horns, his stubby hands working a piece of sandpaper over their rough surface. Every now and then he would hold the horns before him to measure the progress he made, his right, stocky shoulder rising and falling with the even strokes of his hand. Francesco sat opposite him, whittling an oblong piece of wood which was to serve as a base for the horns. Virgillia had taken the oilcloth off the square table and was scrubbing its center, preparing a clean surface for Rosalia who was busily gathering the ingredients to make noodles for the guests. Maria sat opposite the Madonna, with a huge bag of potatoes on her lap, which she was peeling. Signora Derella knocked on the door, then walked in, making herself welcome. Her beady eyes circled the room. She nodded approvingly as Giuseppe and Francesco progressed with the work of the horns.

"Signora Derella, why do you need these horns? Who is going to make you the evil eye?" asked Giuseppe frowning. He had work of his own to do and felt irked with Signora Derella's demands on his limited time.

"Roberto and Bettina can't wait forever to get married. Virgillia must have the evil eye and the horns might work charms and get her a husband."

Virgillia smiled to herself. What excitement she would stir if she shouted, "Ma, pa, Rosalia, Giuseppe, Signora Derella, I have fallen in love, in love, in love. Madly in love." She would too, if she knew that Donald returned her love. Up to now, she had been a lark atop of a Fifth Avenue bus and then she had the unexpected meeting with Donald before the theater. No, she couldn't shout to the world her secret love, because so far, Donald had not even asked her for a date. Who was Meg? Why had Donald placed the Valentine card in his breast pocket over his heart? He could have crumbled it and thrown it away, if it had no meaning for him, she thought jealously.

"Signora Derella, Virgillia doesn't need the horns to help her get a husband. Today Luigi and Salvatore are coming to dinner. Do you remember them?" asked Rosalia as she scattered flour over the surface of the kitchen table. They introduced husbands to Luisa and to me." Signora Derella folded her arms on her narrow chest.

"You see, the horns are working already," she nodded with satisfaction.

"Help me peel potatoes, Signora Derella. Don't sit there idle." Maria handed her the bag of potatoes, a knife and placed a pot for the potatoes at her feet, then she took out the rosary beads from her apron pocket and silently prayed as she glanced at the Madonna.

"Maria puts everyone to work, then she drags out her rope and she mumbles," frowned Signora Derella as she quickly peeled potatoes.

"This rope will get us to heaven, Signora Derella. I am even praying for you." That was the only way Maria could counteract Signora Derella's superstitious belief in the horns, she thought.

"The horns may bring Virgillia a rich husband instead of a poor man like Giuseppe or a hard working carpenter like Ferdinando, Luisa's husband," said Signora Derella.

"Signora Derella, you like to talk nonsense this morning." Francesco grinned amiably as he looked at the base for the horns from every angle as he held it up, away from him.

"If you're not careful, Signora Derella, the horns will also give us Roberto," laughed Giuseppe.

"He isn't rich either, but he is good. As good as Giuseppe." Rosalia patted Giuseppe's shoulder with her flour-smeared hand.

Virgillia moved lightly around the kitchen in a world of her own.

"Virgillia, when are you going to find a sweetheart?" Virgillia energetically cleaned the white enamel of the gas range, glad that they had gotten it in exchange for the old belly stove around which she had spent a lively childhood with ma recounting Bible stories and stories of her childhood in Italy. Now she smiled dreamily at Signora Derella's words.

"Ya, ya, you smile, Virgillia. You had better hurry. Bettina comes next in marriage. She already has a sweetheart, if she behaves," she added darkly.

Virgillia vaguely wondered at herself as she went through the motions preparing her for the great event of meeting Luigi and Salvatore, who in turn would find her a husband. She had dreaded this moment when she knew she would feel as hopeless as the tear stained mourners beating their fists against the closed doors of the hearse, but instead of feeling depressed, she now seemed to feel herself rising above the smugness of the Vina flat, above its anticipated feast. It was foolish to worry about the prospective suitor. It was much easier to think of Donald.

"Would that my heart were within glass shutters" he had murmured. She didn't have to worry about Luigi and Salvatore thrusting an unwanted suitor on her.

Giuseppe had finished his work on the horns. Francesco had pasted them on the smooth piece of wood he had whittled for a base. He had melted a candle in hot oil and with a bit of cloth was passing it over the smooth horns. Rosalia had sewed a new tablecloth and napkins for today's dinner and had Virgillia take out the bastings. Virgillia had pressed them with a damp cloth to retain their newness without creases. Signora Derella had finished peeling the potatoes. She now took the coveted horns and held them gingerly with her fingers. Maria finished praying the rosary. She made the sign of the cross, kissed the beads, and returned them to her pocket. Signora Derella quietly shut the kitchen door after her, giggling with delight over her treasure.

"Franci, Giuseppe, you have used the Lord's day to work on the tool of the devil," admonished Maria. Just then the door opened and Signora Derella, who returned for her shawl which she had left on the chair, heard Maria's remark.

While Francesco, Rosalia, and Giuseppe glanced at Maria in embarrassed silence, Maria calmly said, "Signora Derella, Francesco and Giuseppe have pleased you this morning and now you're going to please me. I want you to come to the mission with me. It starts Monday evening of Lent."

Signora Derella was so pleased with the horns that she was willing to promise Maria anything at the moment.

"Of course I'll come Maria. We're going to be related, aren't we, when Roberto marries Bettina, if Bettina behaves." She ended sourly. After she left, Francesco turned sharply on Maria.

"Maria, you almost made me feel like a fool. Do you want me to drive Signora Derella out and lose Roberto? How could I have refused to work on the horns for her?"

"You helped her belief in the works of the devil, but it might be for the best if she is willing to come to the mission with me. The good Lord will enlighten her, Franci," Maria said with quiet faith.

When the flat was in perfect order for the guests to arrive, Virgillia slipped into her dark blue serge dress with the white organdy collar and cuffs, which she wore to the office on cool days. She had starched a white frilly tea apron and wondered if she should wear it. Francesco, as he put away his tool box, read Virgillia's indecision.

"Wear the apron, Virgillia. Luigi and Salvatore may be better impressed with you."

Rosalia was carefully laying the new tablecloth on the table. She examined Virgillia critically. Virgillia looked pretty and dainty. The apron gave her the domestic touch that Rosalia had seen on girls in magazine advertisements in beautiful, spacious kitchens advertising linoleums.

"Pa, Luigi and Salvatore shouldn't find it hard to get Virgillia a husband, when they see her wearing an apron," agreed Rosalia.

Francesco chuckled.

"The apron looks nice on Virgillia, but I like better the large blue and white striped aprons such as ma wears," said Francesco.

"Pa, please remember it is 1920 now and young girls don't wear striped aprons, which ma has been wearing since the turn of the century," said Virgillia.

"Curb your tongue, Virgillia," said Francesco with a bit of sternness.

Rosalia now joined Maria in the first bedroom to help her mother comb her hair in a more becoming style. Giuseppe had gone to his flat to see what the children were doing. Virgillia busied herself setting the table.

A commotion suddenly sounded in the hall. Heavy

footsteps, loud voices, and a crash against the kitchen door startled Virgillia. Before Francesco could reach the door, it flew open. Bettina and Roberto lay sprawled on the doorstep.

"Bettina, what happened?" Francesco's stern face relaxed. He reprimanded Bettina mildly. Bettina got on her knees but Roberto playfully shoved her away from him. Again Bettina sat on the floor with a thud while Roberto arose and brushed his trousers, holding a photograph behind his back with one hand. Luigi and Salvatore laughed uproariously.

"Is she the daughter who is looking for a sweetheart, Francesco?" asked Luigi in a deep, bass voice, as he pointed to Bettina. He was a tall, stocky man with coal black hair parted on the side, tucked behind large ears. He tweaked his bushy black mustache daintily with thumb and forefinger as he shouted. Salvatore, a slight, weazened man grasped Francesco's hands in greeting, while Luigi bowed low to Rosalia standing in the kitchen.

No, no this would never do, thought Rosalia who now stood in the doorway watching Bettina's fair, girlish sweetness. The gold of her hair brightened the dingy walls of the old corridor.

"Give me that picture, Roberto," ordered Bettina from her squatting position on the floor.

Giuseppe slowly coming upstairs smiled at Bettina's pouting chin, greeting the newcomers by lifting his brows in way of recognition. Bettina was acting outrageously, squatting without dignity on the floor, thought Rosalia looking with annoyance at pa who was busily speaking to his friends. He didn't seem to pay any attention to Bettina. I suppose it's because she looks like ma, Rosalia snorted inwardly.

"Roberto, give me that picture and go away."

Roberto ignored Rosalia's command.

"Bettina, the children are alone downstairs," said Giuseppe quietly, taking the picture from Roberto's hand.

"Bettina is right, Roberto, that is a baby picture taken when she graduated from the eighth grade. I'll take snapshots of her tomorrow, then she'll give you a picture of herself as the young lady she is now," promised Giuseppe.

"Will you?" Roberto asked Bettina eagerly. She nodded. Roberto dusted his trousers, then reached for Bettina's hand and together they raced downstairs laughing merrily.

"Bettina, don't allow Roberto to walk off with anything else," advised Giuseppe as he leaned over the bannister, smiling at the young lovers.

Rosalia sighed with relief. Luigi and Salvatore had been interested in the lovers' quarrel through the running conversation they were having with Francesco. She turned to them now with her best company smile, nodding approvingly to Giuseppe for his wise counselling to the lovers. Her buck teeth shone brilliantly.

"Just children, just children," she explained. "They are childhood sweethearts. They were brought up together right in this hall." Rosalia looked around the kitchen. Now, where was Virgillia? Where did she go? Instead of making herself the center of attraction she had disappeared, leaving the field open to Bettina. Francesco suddenly became aware of Virgillia's absence.

"Virgillia," he called loudly. Maria awoke from her snooze where she had fallen asleep after Rosalia combed her hair. She now came into the kitchen to greet her guests. Rosalia had told Francesco time and again to entertain his friends in the parlor but he preferred the kitchen. The informality of the kitchen made conversation easier.

"I am glad we only meet on cheerful occasions, such as matrimony," smiled Maria by way of welcome.

Virgillia stood framed in the doorway of the first bedroom with a tray bearing glasses and a bottle of cordial.

Francesco nodded approval of Virgillia's thoughtfulness

and even Rosalia felt all was not yet lost with Virgillia. At least she knew the rules of ettiquette.

"Virgillia, meet my good friends Luigi and Salvatore." Francesco bowed slightly before his guests. The men stared at Virgillia for a long moment. Francesco felt uncomfortable. What did his friends think of Virgillia? Did they know of a nice young man who would be attracted to her? His friends' words dispelled his fears for Virgillia's future.

"Francesco, wasn't Virgillia that little, thin dark girl who was the flower girl for Luisa?" asked Salvatore, eyeing Virgillia with unconcealed admiration.

"My, my. Virgillia has grown into a beautiful girl, Francesco!" stated Luigi, ogling her with his large, black eyes. Virgillia blushed as she passed the cordial.

Francesco spread out his palms and lifted his chin in the air several times as though he was begging for an answer. His friends understood. They nodded. They would comply with his request of finding a suitable sweetheart for Virgillia.

"Francesco, do you remember the Longobardo family who lived in the big mansion on the side of the mountain in our village of Itri in Italy?" asked Luigi.

Francesco and Maria nodded.

"My mother used to wash Signora Longobardo's clothes in the stream below our home," remembered Maria. "They were the aristocracy. Why do you ask?" questioned Maria curiously.

"Do you know that after we left our village, twenty-five years ago, the Longobardos lost their fortune? They too came to America."

Francesco and Maria were surprised. Francesco crossed his legs impatiently. They had seated themselves in a semicircle in the kitchen. Luigi and Salvatore were getting off the subject of finding a suitor for Virgillia. Who cared about the Longobardos, thought Francesco. Salvatore's next words had Francesco sitting on the edge of his chair.

"The Longobardos lived for a while in Manhattan, then moved to another state. I know they had a son. A few years ago I met them at the Festa Della Madonna Della Civita social. It was the year when you were sick with fever and didn't come to the festa, Francesco. That son of the Longobardos would be just fine for Virgillia." Luigi toyed with his mustache, looking from Maria to Francesco.

Maria stared incredulously at their friends.

"Are you mad?" she exclaimed in an awed voice. "In Italy the Longobardos were noblemen. They would never stoop to marry a Vina." Luigi and Salvatore laughed.

"Maria, there is no class distinction in America. Everyone is free and equal." Salvatore tried to sound convincing but Maria shook her head, feeling sad that the good men could not find Virgillia a husband.

"Impossible that a Longobardo will marry a Vina, even in America where there is no class distinction. The Longobardos know us from Italy. We were peasants, people of the soil, uneducated and illiterate," she stated firmly, as she looked crestfallen at Francesco.

"When will we see this fellow? When will we have the honor of meeting him?" asked Francesco with equal misgivings and a hint of sarcasm. He wanted Virgillia to meet a simple fellow like Giuseppe or Ferdinando. Someone on their own level. Virgillia made life difficult for him, even when he tried to help her. His friends were going over his head in thinking of a suitor above their station in life, but Francesco had no choice.

Luigi's next words brought further disillusionment to Francesco.

"You have to give us a little time Francesco. I know they used to live in New York City. Probably they moved to Rhode Island, where most of our countrymen migrated. We'll make a special trip and try to find them." Luigi looked into space with a baffled expression on his face.

"I'm sure we'll locate them," said Salvatore. He sensed Francesco and Maria's disappointment. Maria and Francesco were not pleased with their friend's vagueness regarding Virgillia's suitor.

Virgillia who had gathered the empty cordial glasses on the tray, now tapped her mother's shoulder and beckoned to her.

"Excuse me, please. I want to get my crocheting," said Maria as she followed Virgillia to the parlor.

Maria sat gingerly on the sofa. She graced the parlor sofa on ceremonious ocassions, being too busy in the kitchen throughout the year to enjoy the comfortable seat. Now she sat with her hands on her knees looking inquiringly at Virgillia who paced the parlor floor restlessly.

"Sit down, Virgillia. You make my head swim. Has anything happened?" she asked faintly disturbed at Virgillia's set lips.

"Ma, this is ridiculous. I don't want Luigi and Salvatore to find me a husband."

"Virgie, you frightened me. I thought you didn't feel well. You are much too modest Virgie. Too modest. I don't see why pa is afraid you'll get in trouble with strange men." She spoke half to herself. "Povera figlia," Maria looked compassionately at her least understood daughter.

Virgillia shrugged her shoulders and turned to the window helplessly.

"Virgie, please get me the bedspread. I can't bend." Virgillia got on her knees and dragged the cardboard box from underneath the sofa where Maria kept it. Virgillia resumed her position before the window as Maria contentedly crocheted. Every once in a while she would look toward Virgillia. Francesco was right indeed. Virgillia was a difficult girl to understand. What was wrong if their friends found her a suitor? Wasn't marriage the best career for most women? Had not God ordered everyone to go into the ark two by two? Wasn't Virgillia interested in marriage? Maria asked herself. A devoted husband like Francesco, a home full of children would keep a woman busy and happy for years. It would also keep her safe from getting into mischief, once she made her committment to God, Maria thought wisely.

"Virgillia, Virgillia." Virgillia continued to stare at her world from the square of window pane, even though she heard Rosalia's agitated voice calling her. Maria quickly returned her work to the box.

"Wake up, Virgi. Rosalia is calling you. Don't you smell the tomato sauce on the homemade noodles?" Maria's mouth watered. Rosalia now draped the doorway, her hands on her hips. Although she had tried to make her voice sound casual, her nose inflated angrily.

"Virgillia says she doesn't want our friends to find her a husband. I don't know what she's got on her mind, Rosalia," said Maria helplessly.

"Don't worry, Virgillia. They took one look at you and they find they haven't got anyone to match you with." Rosalia spoke disparagingly.

"You're wrong, Rosalia." Maria was quick to defend Virgillia. "Didn't you hear they want her to meet a signore?"

"Don't you believe it, ma. They are only trying to be nice," said Rosalia scornfully.

Maria puckered her face like a baby about to cry.

For once Virgillia hoped that Rosalia's surmise would prove correct. She took a deep breath, then slowly expelled it.

"Maria, Rosalia, Virgillia!" Francesco's commanding voice boomed from the kitchen.

"Quick, ma, pa is getting hungry. Hurry, Virgillia." Rosalia adjusted her hands on her hips, walking in her best company manner, swinging her shoulders gawkily. Maria followed, her face flushed.

Francesco was clamoring for his dinner and he had to have it on the dot of one. Well, that is what happened when she did not supervise the meal, she thought. Virgillia wound up the file down the aisle taking small, impatient steps to match her mother's slow walk.

The men had seated themselves. Franceso was waving his nervous hands as he stressed his arguments. Luigi with large knuckles beat the table as he spoke, tinkling the glasses. Salvatore sat quietly at the table watching the wine bottle. When would Francesco pass the wine? Salvatore liked wine. When he drank it, it made him feel colossal.

"Let's drink a toast to Virgillia," he suggested, as the women found their seats around the table. Francesco agreed, uncorking the wine bottle.

"Salutti," everyone pointed their glasses at Virgillia, then slowly drained them. Virgillia felt uncomfortable. Guiseppe looked at her kindly.

Amid much merriment and clatter of dishes the meal progressed smoothly. Rosalia kept a steady stream of conversation. She spoke of the dresses she and Virgillia should make for the children for the Festa Della Madonna Della Civita social on July twenty-first. The Festa Della Madonna turned the conversation again to the Longobardos. This time they would make sure they would be at the social with their son, Luigi and Salvatore both affirmed, as their glances appraised Virgillia. With each affirmation their wine glasses were refilled. Luigi now spoke of their life in Italy.

"Francesco, do you remember the wonderful serenade you brought to Maria?" Maria flushed happily at being remembered in the midst of Virgillia's coming romance. Virgillia had never heard about the serenade and giggled at the thought of pa serenading ma.

Luigi and Salvatore turned to her.

"Those were our years of romance and music, Virgillia.

90

Wouldn't you like to be serenaded?" asked Salvatore, winking mischievously at Francesco.

Virgillia laughed at the incongruous setting of their flat.

"Don't you need a window and a moon?" she asked.

"A guitar and a good love song is enough, Virgillia." Luigi's booming laughter filled the room.

"One moment, please," Salvatore lifted a thin finger. "We also need a very beautiful woman, whom we have." He pointed to Virgillia. Virgillia blushed.

"You all forgot some very good wine to go with the music, the guitar and the beautiful woman." Francesco happily filled all the empty glasses on the table.

Maria soon lost herself in one of her impromptu naps. The door opened and Tommy sailed into the room in her most grown-up manner. Her blonde, strawlike hair was parted in the center and combed behind her ears. To get a real sheen to her hair, Tommy had placed her head under the open water faucet, soaking it. The water gave it the right dark touch of color which Tommy liked. As she approached Rosalia, she flattened her small chin, puckered her lips together and inflated the nostrils of her small nose. She raised her shoulders to appear tall and lined her forehead with boredom, in precise imitation of an annoyed prima donna. She gave a few running steps, without losing her pose, in order to reach Rosalia's chair before pa's questioning stare would put itself into words. An old discarded organdy collar floated around her thin neck above her tightly buttoned, shabby red coat. Francesco was about to address her, when she hurriedly grasped Rosalia's ear and buried her lips, with a command in its depths. Rosalia frowned, then catching her father's eager stare and the guest's inquisitive expressions, she smiled disarmingly.

"All right Tommy, all right!" Rosalia fumed inwardly but that was Tommy, mischievous and clever to further her own interests. All through her stay in Rosalia's flat, Tommy had watched the clock. Patiently she had waited. She knew that any festivities in the Vina flat lagged at three o'clock. That was sufficient time to whisper a little command in Rosalia's ear and ample time for all the children to enjoy the movie around the corner. Tommy had been warned more than once not to try her high powered blackmailing tactics when company was being entertained, but Tommy knew Rosalia would not disgrace her publicly. That would be a direct reflection on her family's behavior and by the time the last guest departed, everyone was too busy discussing this and that to bother much about her.

"Guiseppe, go downstairs to our flat. See what the children are doing and give Tommy what she wants." Giuseppe and Rosalia exchanged understanding glances. Giuseppe carefully edged his way out of the tiny space afforded by Maria's chair and the gas range, not wishing to disturb Maria's nap. His short knotted fingers tweaked Tommy's ear as he pushed her toward the door. Tommy forgot her dignity and worldly ambitions to appear sensational and yelled wildly when Giuseppe gave her a slight shove. Playfully he shut her mouth. Tommy pummeled him, boy fashion. Tommy never resented Giuseppe because, like Bettina, she could use him on occasions, as she was now doing.

The door closed on Giuseppe's round, lazy-eyed face and Tommy's wild, laughing screams.

Maria continued to doze. She would soon lend gentle snores to the air pungent with savory odors, tinkling glasses and words, words, words. They heard the clickity clack of Signora Derella's heels. She flitted quietly into the room. The hours dragged. The yellow gaslight swam around Virgillia, Luigi's massive shoulders, Salvatore sneaking a glass of wine, Francesco, dominant and masterful, sitting at the head of the table, directing Virgillia's destiny, Signora Derella's high, cackling laugh as she accepted Francesco's glass of wine. Through this whirling sea of futility, Virgillia caught

Giuseppe's kind, compassionate eyes, as he took his seat after returning to the flat. She saw her mother's childish simplicity and unconcern for the tensions of the world around her, as she gently snoozed and Virgillia felt strengthened. She groped for thoughts of Donald, but the immediate events took complete control of her mind and senses.

"Salutti, salutti a tutti!" Signora Derella smacked her lips. She glanced at the company and thought of her horns on her mantlepiece. They must be working for Virgillia, she thought gleefully. It wouldn't be long before Roberto married Bettina, if Bettina behaved.

TEN

Maria had dragged Signora Derella to the mission with tongue in cheek. During Lent, she had promised herself that she would bring Bettina's future mother-in-law back to her senses, for Bettina's sake. The mission might open her mind to the fact that God is the only reality in the world. Everything withers and dies and is passing. Signora Derella must understand that God must be worshipped above everyone and everything on earth, even above a silly thing like a cow's horns. Signora Derella, however, did not intend to make Maria's task easy. She plagued Maria with many questions, when after the mission, she followed Maria to the Vina kitchen to share a cup of espresso coffee. The Vinas drank espresso coffee with a bit of anise cordial after a hearty meal, to help the digestion. Brown coffee was not used in Italy up to the time that Francesco and Maria lived there. Espresso coffee was roasted in a manner where the caffeine was entirely taken out of the coffee bean and was not harmful to the nerves, said Francesco. He had to walk several miles to Mott Street to buy the espresso coffee roasted Italian style in the Italian market place. For the nine days of the mission, Maria allowed herself the treat of a demitasse while she hassled with Signora Derella's perverted mind.

The missionary priest who came especially for the Lenten mission roared about heaven and hell as though he had been there and had just returned, but Signora Derella did not question his statements. It was to Maria that she brought her many doubts and assertions, even though the missionary priest begged the parishioners to come to him with their doubts in confession.

"Why should I listen to him, Maria," Signora Derella challenged Maria one evening, toward the end of the mission, as she slowly sipped her coffee from a demitasse cup.

Maria looked helplessly at Signora Derella, then turned her gaze towards Francesco for help. He was leaning over a large board which he placed on the old sewing machine beneath the picture of the Madonna. Weeks before Christmas Francesco would recreate the manger scene with the infant Jesus lying on a bed of straw in a stable with the wise men and sheep at the door. When the plaster figures broke, he fixed them. One of the wise men once lost his hand. Francesco fashioned a new hand holding a large sausage, painted it red as a gift to the new born infant. Another wise man lost his head. Francesco made a new head with a pumpkin on it. It seemed the wise men grew wiser after Francesco got through with them. The children roared with laughter at the wise men, who with a little plaster and paint were renewed. Now with Easter approaching, Francesco took the large statue of Jesus that Maria kept on the bureau in her bedroom. The statue had its palms uplifted in blessing. Francesco was busily fastening two bright, red flags with gold crosses made of tinsel material sewed in their center to the hands of the statue, to signify the resurrection on Easter morning. The children saved their pennies during Lent to buy fresh flowers, making a garden of lillies about the risen Christ on Easter morning.

Maria now looked at the Madonna.

"Dear Mother," she prayed silently, "give me the grace to help Signora Derella place her trust and faith in God." Maria felt that Signora Derella drained her. She breathed heavily. Francesco hearing Maria gasp for breath looked with annoyance at Signora Derella.

"Signora Derella, if it makes you happier to have faith in your horns instead of God, do as you please."

Maria looked reprovingly at Francesco.

"Have another cup of coffee, Signora Derella. I made it stronger tonight. After the mission is over, you'll go to confession. The missionary priest will answer all the questions I cannot answer, Signora Derella." Maria spoke slowly, soothingly, as though speaking to an ailing child.

"I'll have to make up my mind, Maria." Signora Derella smacked her lips as she sipped the coffee.

"The coffee is good and strong Maria. It is good and strong as you are," Signora Derella said thoughtfully.

Rosalia had spent a few hours at the shoe shine parlor to add the day's receipts. She heard Signora Derella's words when she entered the kitchen.

"Ma's roasted chestnuts used to make us listen to her stories when we were children, Signora Derella. They tasted good and ma's espresso coffee tastes good too. If you listen to ma, your heart will fill with God's peace." Rosalia poured a cup of coffee for herself and refilled Signora Derella's cup adding an extra drop of anise cordial in it. Poor soul, she needed warmth and kindness after losing her husband, thought Rosalia.

Virgillia and the children now clattered upstairs, their arms filled with pressed clothes. During the mission Maria had asked the children to stay in Rosalia's flat until after she had her coffee with Signora Derella and Francesco. Virgillia didn't mind. Rosalia's children fell quickly asleep after their active day. Tommy, Caterina, and Angie did their homework in the parlor, and she either helped ma, pressing the family clothes, or took care of her personal needs. The Vinas never found time heavy on their hands.

"Perhaps I should pray that Luigi and Salvatore will bring Virgillia a nice suitor?" Signora Derella said slowly as she clickety clacked out of the room.

Signora Derella's promise fell on deaf ears, for Virgillia was tired. She wanted to retire early and think of Donald. The firm was expanding so quickly that there were rumors of enlarging their Boston office. Their work had doubled in the new office, with the result that the week following their happy meeting when they saw *Glass Shutters*, Virgillia only heard Donald's voice when he buzzed her for files. All other hours seemed to be taken with conferences in or out of his office. The directors took up his time during lunch hours. But was Donald even remotely interested in her? Virgillia asked herself.

Donald too wondered about Virgillia. He had wanted to date Virgillia some evening after office hours, but his mother became suddenly interested in his welfare. Mothers are angels but sometimes they become downright impossible, he confided to Ben. "The farm ran itself," said Ben, and that is why she invited herself to stay in the city in Donald's apartment for a spell. Donald felt irked because he thought his mother was exaggerating her eagerness to balm his ego after Meg left him. Now she was also asking him to attend affairs with her and dad, so he could more quickly forget Margaret. Preposterous, thought Donald.

His mother insisted that he was becoming a machine. He rarely visited the farm on weekends since Margaret left him. Donald only seemed to have time for work, work and more work, she teased. She suggested that he round out his social life. She told Ben that Donald was becoming warped, self-centered.

Donald had always humored his parents, but now they were coming between him and his plans for Virgillia. His mother insisted on making the theater rounds with him during the evening and he had to grin and bear it, because his mother thought she was doing him good. After Mrs. Long stayed a week in the apartment, even Ben Worth laughed inwardly at Donald, who seemed to be tied to his mother's apron strings.

"Donald likes his women capable, mature, settled," said Ben while Mrs. Long laughed not knowing the jibe was directed at her.

If he could tell his mother that he had fallen in love again. If he could only tell her that he had never been in love with Margaret. He had been over ambitious for his own ends. Virgillia had shown him the difference. He knew his mother would understand and be very happy with his new love, but he had not asked Virgillia for a date. Would she accept? he wondered. They had explored New York City together only because they had a half-day off from the office and then he had casually met her outside the theater. Why did she have two passes in her bag? Had she quarreled with her boyfriend?

He was anxious to get back to the office. The week before he had spent in conferences and more conferences. It seemed there had never seen such a building boom as now. The end of the first world war had found low income families with a surplus of money earned in war plants. It seemed as though people wanted to lift themselves out of cold water flats and buy steamheated houses, and they all seemed to want them at once.

Architects were in demand. He should have been very happy in his career, but his heart during the loneliness of the evening and night craved the warmth and companionship of a young, eager girl with rounded olive cheeks and a dimpled chin.

After his mother left, buoyantly he went to the office, anxious to date Virgillia for an evening. He found a note on his desk. Impatiently he snapped his fingers and pursed his lips. He left the office immediately.

When Virgillia arrived at nine o'clock, she picked up the note that Donald had left for her.

It is imperative for me to be in the Boston office this morning. Took an early plane. Hope to return Monday. Have a nice weekend.

Donald

Vacant hours, vacant days with Donald in Boston. In her heart welled a void. Disappointment and love didn't mix well, like oil and water, the two substances were there, neither doing anything for the other.

ELEVEN

It was Saturday. Donald was still in Boston. Francesco was seated on the window sill. His feet rested on the fire escape. He had bought a new batch of mint and basil plants and was setting them in small, earthen pots. When the plants strengthened, he transplanted them to his large, wooden flower boxes against the wall of the tenement. During autumn, Maria would snip the mint and basil leaves, dry and store them in glass jars, flavoring her cooking with them throughout the year. While busy at his task, Francesco would turn his head from time to time ·with his eyes squinting from the sun toward the kitchen sink where Tommy was clattering dishes in a huge pan of suds. Tommy's few leisure hours after school had been surprised by Francesco's early arrival. She couldn't understand why pa had come home early. She strained her ears to catch some word that would answer her question, which she, in turn, would trade for a few pennies with Virgillia, but all she heard were whispers and Maria's asthmatic, punctuated laughter. On his arrival from the factory, Francesco had led Tommy to the stacked dishes. Tommy had no alternative. She had planned for a whole week to see a movie. Today she felt like disturbing someone for her frustration in missing her favorite treat.

Tommy couldn't even understand why pa had breathlessly lugged several dust-laden bottles of wine from the cellar. They were now resting in the washtub. She could hear the swift, cold running water cooling them. The Vinas had invented their own cooling system during weather when the extra item of ice could be dispensed. A large dish of shelled roasted nuts was hidden in the lower compartment of the gas range. The kitchen table had been pushed near the window where Francesco was seated and Maria was filling little squares of dough with an egg, cheese, and sugar mixture. Frying the delicacies was an ordeal in the hot, disordered kitchen with spring rapidly approaching summer. The table close to the window gave Maria a breath of air, plus the distraction of conversing with Francesco.

"Povera figlia," Maria was murmuring to Francesco. "Virgie is just a modest girl. Sometimes you just don't understand her, Franci."

Francesco's wide, thin lips opened to a grin. Perhaps he was a little too harsh with Virgillia. His eagle eyes darted from Tommy, washing dishes, to Caterina seated on a low bench before a chair solemnly doing her homework. The catechism and her rosary were beside her. Of all the children Caterina was most devoted to prayer. Maria and Francesco secretly hoped that one of their children would be given the grace to serve God, willingly relinquishing the world to embrace a religious vocation. They hoped Caterina would fulfill their hope. Angie was a baby. They wouldn't have to worry about her for years to come. Francesco had no scruples regarding Bettina. She was too much like Maria to get in trouble of her owm making. With ease she had fallen in love with Roberto, saving him anxiety and worries regarding the choice of a husband. Her generous heart had enough love to share with Roberto and his difficult mother. Of course he knew Tommy, though a bit mischievous at times, was very clever. She should do good for herself. She took what she wanted from life and that is how she would get a husband too. Francesco grinned to himself. He was happy now that he had christened her with his father's name, Tomaso, Tomasina Vina. God had made him feel that there would be no boys in his family and Tommy had looked so much like a boy when she was born that he had unhesitatingly named her after his father, knowing that in heaven he would be very happy to know that he had not been forgotten on earth. If only Francesco could get Virgillia married, he would indeed feel he had accomplished his duty to his Maker.

"Let me taste one of those cheesecakes, Maria. Let me see if they are too sweat or just right."

Maria handed one cheesecake to Francesco with smiling satisfaction. Francesco sometimes was sparing in his praise of her cooking, but in her heart she knew that he appreciated her superb culinary efforts. His expression of contentment after a meal was all the thanks Maria desired. Now he smacked his thin lips.

"Put them in a safe place, Maria, or the children will finish them before the night is over."

"That's enough, that's enough Tommy. Don't eat the cheesecakes with your eyes." Maria handed a chubby cake to Tommy and one to Caterina.

Now it was time for Francesco to water his fire escape plantation. He searched for the old tea kettle under the washtub's curtained recess. Tommy stood aside as her father filled the kettle with water, eating her cake with gusto, watching Caterina's small, bent figure over her copy book, greedily looking at the untouched cheesecake at her elbow. Her eyes kindled mischievously. The moment to strike for her disappointment of forfeiting her movie arrived.

"Pa, you tell me not to use a lot of ink when I do homework. Look at Caterina." Francesco looked over Caterina's shoulder, holding his water filled kettle with both hands. Hurriedly he reached the fire escape, rested his heavy burden, then hustled back to Caterina.

"That's enough, now, Caterina! What can you learn from that?" Caterina looked up solemnly, confidently.

"That's Palmer Movement, pa. Teacher told me to do it for homework." Caterina's hand moved around and around as the pen and ink sped large circles across the page.

"Funny, teacher never told me to do that for homework."

Tommy put one foot forward, one hand on her hip swinging herself back and forth as she continued to lick the fingers of her free hand.

"Tell teacher to give you reading and writing homework, Caterina. You're only wasting ink." Caterina felt hurt and humiliated that pa didn't understand that she had to do Palmer Movement to train herself for more legible writing. Caterina saw Tommy greedily looking at her cheese cake and knew that she had confused pa about her home work, so that in the excitement of battling pa, Tommy would take the cake. Caterina did not like the cheesecakes and would have gladly given her cake to Tommy. Why did Tommy have to plan all her campaigns like a general to achieve her ends, thought Caterina sadly.

Caterina's being, young as she was, seemed fused with understanding. Now her eyes met those of her heavenly Mother. The Madonna's sweet face looked down on her from the golden frame hanging over the kitchen wall.

"Make me like you, dear Mother, good and pure." Caterina's heart prayed fervently. "Make me gentle, but above all, give me patience." She picked up her books, rosary and catechism, then opened the kitchen door and quietly went downstairs to Rosalia's flat. Before she closed the door she saw Tommy's greedy eyes and victorious smile, as she furtively took the cheesecake from the chair. Caterina's eyes filled with tears. Why was Tommy greedy, self-indulgent, hurting others to satisfy herself.

"Maria, Caterina doesn't say too much. Sometimes I wish she would answer me, even fight back. Was Virgillia like her at her age?" Francesco climbed through the window to the fire escape.

"God wants you to live one minute at a time, Franci. Don't look back and don't look forward," said Maria catching Francesco's anxious expression. "I don't remember Virgillia walking around with a rosary and a catechism in her hand, the way

Caterina does. Try to live every moment to the very best of your ability, Franci, then leave the rest to God," soothed Maria. They both smiled as Tommy innocently crunched Caterina's cheesecake, licking her lips with unusual gusto.

While Caterina's almost perfect soul was coping with Tommy's imperfections, Virgillia coming home from the office walked slowly upstairs. Rosalia's kitchen door was open.

"Come in, Virgie." Rosalia came to the door. Virgillia searched her sister's face for the secret in her voice, then looked with surprise at the huge grip on the kitchen floor. She could hear Angie, Nicky, and Nanny playing "wing awound awosy" in the parlor. Rosalia, her thick fuzzy hair at loose ends, looked at the grip and at Virgillia, her eyes shining with suppressed excitement.

"Why are you packing, Rosalia?"

"Didn't you know, Virgillia?" Virgillia stared vacantly at the grip for several seconds, then her face paled.

"Is ma going to Cousin Marietta again, Rosalia?"

"Yes, Virgillia. Ma is so round you can't tell she is pregnant. Shh—don't let the children hear, not yet, anyway!"

"Oh, my goodness," Virgillia uttered helplessly.

"I hope it will be a boy this time, Virgillia. You know how the neighbors laugh at ma for having a regiment of girls."

Rosalia clasped Virgillia's cold hands and looked at her speechless face.

"I, I thought Angie would be the last?" whispered Virgillia.

"It's a shame to bother Cousin Marietta now that the weather is getting warm, but God wills children, Virgillia." Virgillia put on one of Rosalia's faded kimonos and helped stuff the grip with preserved eggplants, peppers, and several bottles of homemade wine. Cousin Marietta liked the Vina preserves and homemade wine.

"When is ma going?" asked Virgillia.

104

"Saturday or Sunday." Rosalia dragged another grip from under the bed.

"We'll put Angie's baby clothes and the diapers that ma saved in this one." Rosalia rambled on while Virgillia worried. Last time when ma went to Cousin Marietta, Signora Derella had kept an eye on the Vina menage. Virgillia had a hard time. Signora Derella was always scolding. She expected every chair to stay in its place as in her flat where there were no children and she was forever hiding the bread from the children. Ma kept a clean white pillowcase hanging behind the kitchen door. The pillowcase held long, fresh loaves of Italian bread which an Italian baker delivered every morning. After school ma always gave the children a large piece of bread cut in the center, filled with sliced tomato, olive oil, oregano, minced garlic, and salt to taste. It was a delicious tasting sandwich, like an uncooked pizza. Tommy called it an Italian heroine, being there were only girls in the Vina family.

Signora Derella used to hide the pillowcase with the bread in her kitchen and sliced it so thin that, as Giuseppe said, she served it like the host in Holy Communion. Rosalia always went to care for ma while Giuseppe kept an eye on the children during the evening. The last time ma went, Virgillia was in high school and was able to take care of the children after school. Now, more than ever, she didn't want Signora Derella poking her nose in the Vina affairs, thought Virgillia.

"You're going with ma, of course," stated Virgillia. A shadow crossed Rosalia's face. "Pa wants to come too this time. Poor pa he wants to know if it is a boy right away. I don't blame him for being impatient after seven girls."

"It's another child whichever way you look at it," said Virgillia. She was spared Rosalia's opinion of her practical viewpoint by the sudden opening of the kitchen door. Caterina's large eyes were brilliant with tears, her small mouth was tightly shut, drooping at the corners.

"Well, what happened now?" bristled Rosalia.

Running downstairs, Caterina knew she would find scolding Rosalia. She had not expected to see Virgillia. Now she smiled through her tears. In the crook of Virgillia's arm she slowly related her experience with pa and Tommy who ate her cheesecake.

"I'm sure it's here, Caterina." Caterina sat on the edge of the chair hopefully watching Virgillia searching in her handbag. At last Virgillia found it, a plain black fountain pen adorned with a gold band. It had been Virgillia's high school graduation gift. A pleased smile lit Caterina's sombre eyes.

"Do all the Palmer Movement you please," encouraged Virgillia. Caterina spread her copybook on the kitchen table and went to work. Virgillia now turned to Rosalia who was kneeling before the grips, folding baby clothes. Rosalia was shaking her head disapprovingly.

"Virgillia, you mustn't approve of Caterina's disobedience. She may grow up giving us a hard time, same as you." Rosalia sighed.

"I'm having a much harder time, Rosalia, trying to convince everyone that I don't want to be matched to a husband," Virgillia answered dryly, "but that's life, I suppose. Life is a checkerboard, and everyone moves as his or her mind wants to move, even if it hurts another," she finished philosophically.

Virgillia and Rosalia had many intimate talks and rarely agreed, yet they seldom became offensive. Virgillia appreciated the shallow depths of Rosalia's mind and her generosity to ma's family. Rosalia pitied Virgillia who had advanced to womanhood with an immature mind, yet their private opinions of each other did not mar the bond of sisterly affection that held them together.

"I told ma we'll have supper here so she can rest this evening," said Rosalia, her voice filled with concern for her mother.

"Are we going to have cheesecakes too?" asked Caterina,

deciding to give her share to Virgillia whom she loved above all her sisters.

"Rosalia, what is Caterina talking about. She mentioned cheesecakes before. Ma only makes them for special company. Who is coming?" Virgillia's curiosity was now fully aroused.

"Aw, Virgie, Caterina doesn't know what she is talking about." Rosalia avoided Virgillia's glance as she nervously unfolded and folded the baby clothes, then added, "Ma must be frying cauliflower dipped in batter. Come, let's prepare supper." Rosalia was anxious to change the subject.

It was past ten o'clock when Rosalia and Virgillia completed the preparation for Maria's departure. They had discussed the inadvisability of having Signora Derella supervising the household because of the added problem of Bettina working evening hours.

"Let's write and ask Luisa to come and stay with us several weeks," suggested Virgillia hopefully.

"We could do that, but you know how she travels around with her husband, Virgillia."

Virgillia slipped a paper from Caterina's copy book and wrote Luisa an urgent plea to visit the family.

After supper the children had gathered once more in the parlor to play their game of "wing awound awosy," but their full stomachs demanding surplus energy reduced them to a deep sleep, in a heap on the floor. Caterina had dutifully washed the dishes, cleared the kitchen table, then resumed the liberty of doing her handwriting exercises.

When Virgillia returned to her flat upstairs she carried sleeping Angie, while Caterina tugged her skirt in the dim gas-lit hall. Slowly they climbed the stairs. When the neighbors laughed at the ease with which the Vinas coped with their problems, Rosalia joined in their laughter and said the Vinas did not have problems, because they lived right through them. Francesco agreed, saying it felt easier if you rolled along with them. Virgillia now thought of these statements as she heard swift running footsteps on the floor below. They sounded like Bettina's footsteps. Soon Bettina appeared and hurried past her.

"Let me through, Virgie, let me through before Signora Derella sees me." Bettina opened the kitchen door and rushed into the bedroom where she quickly undressed. A hurried shuffling brought Virgillia and the children into the kitchen.

"What's the matter with Bettina?" asked Francesco.

"Signora Derella is coming upstairs after Bettina."

"Madonna mia," exclaimed Maria patiently, "be kind to Signora Derella's mind," she prayed.

"Take out the gaslight and go to bed at once," ordered Francesco in a loud whisper.

Within the next few seconds the Vina girls had all scampered to bed. Even though Bettina had eaten no supper she soon fell asleep.

Virgillia tucked Caterina and Angie in bed for the night and found Tommy sleeping carefree. Beneath the light blanket Virgillia saw a searchlight, a western story magazine pilfered from Roberto's collection and the unusual delicacy of cheesecakes. Caterina was right, thought Virgillia.

"Tommy is a cheat," said Caterina without malice.

"Life will teach her, Caterina, if her family and Father Ignatius make no dent on her mind." Virgillia whispered as she shook her head, wondering why pa thought Tommy presented no problem.

Virgillia heard the hushed tones of her folks in the darkness of the kitchen. She heard Signora Derella's insistent knock on the kitchen door, which no one acknowledged.

Lying on her back, wedged between her sisters, Virgillia was puzzled. Her mother had made the cheesecakes. For what occasion? The cakes could not be for Cousin Marietta, because ma wouldn't make them Wednesday, if she was leaving on Saturday or Sunday.

TWELVE

Virgillia fell into a fitful sleep. Donald persisted in her dreams. Rosalia was laughing scornfully at her. Donald's deep blue eyes held Virgillia's glance. He came toward her. She felt pleasure, irresistable pleasure at his touch until pa came between her and Donald. Then pa laughed loudly. Rosalia joined in his laughter. It was a strident laughter that jarred Virgillia's nerves. They laughed louder and louder. Pa then reached for her shoulder and shook her. She reached for Donald's hand, but she could not find it. At the thought of losing Donald, she summoned all her strength and screamed.

"Wake up, Virgie, wake up!"

Virgillia sat up in bed. A jangle of discordant music filled the air. There was loud laughter too. Someone was shaking her shoulder.

"Wake up, Virgie. You screamed. You must have had a nightmare. Try not to awaken the children. Luigi and Salvatore have brought you a serenade and the parents of the fellow they want you to meet," Rosalia whispered, her eyes bulging with excitement.

Virgillia pressed her fingers to her ears and slumped back on her pillow. This was even worse than the nightmare, she thought. Rosalia stood with her arms folded on her chest, waiting for Virgillia to get up and receive her company. The jangle of music tried to play the melody of "O Maria, O Maria." The familiar words filled the air. Many voices accompanied the music, accentuating the phrases that were meant for Virgillia. They repeated the refrain, substituting, "O Virgie, O Virgie," for "O Maria, O Maria." Virgillia felt a deep resentment. Why were they serenading her? Bettina had the lover. Why didn't they play for Bettina? Over and over they sang,

> O Virgie, O Virgie
> O let me sleep, embraced in your loving arms
>
> O Virgie, O Virgie
> How much sleep have I lost over you
> Please let me sleep
> O Virgie, O Virgie!

Virgillia's face burned. Rosalia's lips curled with anger at Virgillia's indifference.

"Get dressd quickly, Virgie, and don't forget your very best smile for the company," Rosalia hissed the information.

"Luigi and Salvatore didn't bring the young man to meet Virgillia. They brought his mother and father to meet you. I hope you make a good impression on them."

After giving her orders Rosalia ran towards the kitchen, not to miss any of the festivities. Virgillia heard the opening of the door, Francesco's happy voice, Maria's chuckling. It was indeed an honor for the Vinas to have a daughter serended in Italian fashion in the presence of the Longobardos, who in their Italian village would not stoop to speak to a Vina. Virgillia heard Luigi's booming voice offering congratulations to the sleepy Juliet, the thin piping voice of Salvatore suggesting they all drink to the bride to be. Virgillia wondered who strummed the guitar and was surprised, as she peeked through the curtained window that separated the first bedroom from the kitchen, to see pa strumming the guitar just the way he must have done when he was a gay young blade in Italy. The boards of the bed creaked and Virgillia ran back to the bedroom. She found Tommy sitting up.

"What's all the noise?" she asked rubbing her eyes.

"Hush, Tommy, don't let the children awake. It's a serenade, Italian style."

"O Virgie, it's too, too wonderful. A real serenade!"

She looked up at Virgillia and from the reflection of the vigil light burning before the statue of Saint Theresa on their bureau, Virgillia didn't appear to be happy. Tommy thought she seemed very much distressed.

"If only we had a window to see the moon, it would be perfect, Virgie." Tommy flung her arms in the air, trying to soften her boyish voice. Virgillia couldn't help smiling. Tommy was an ugly duckling, awkward but cocksure, she thought.

"Stop waving your arms and go to sleep, Tommy, or you'll start a serenade in here."

Bettina stirred, opened her eyes. "Is it morning?" she asked alarmed. "Has Signora Derella seen me?"

"No, Bettina." Virgillia spoke gently.

"That's Virgillia's serenade, silly. Isn't it a dream, Bettina?" Bettina pressed her fingers in her ears. She was sleepy. She closed her eyes and fell asleep again.

Virgillia had completed her toilette as best she could in the half-lit room. She stood timidly in the doorway several minutes before Rosalia saw her. Mr. Longobardo was now strumming the guitar. He smiled at her. Virgillia was surprised. She liked Mr. Longobardo at once. He was a tall, rugged man with a slight stoop to his shoulders. His face was deeply lined but the lines gave strength, not age, to his square face. His black hair was slightly gray at the temples. His wife sitting beside Maria at the table was a well-kept woman with silver hair and a good figure, though slightly plump. Her chin was molded in stern lines, which disappeared when she smiled. Virgillia thought it was a charming smile, dispelling the seriousness of her face. She now bent her head to the side as her blue eyes appraised Virgillia. Virgillia sensed that the Longobardos seemed highly amused with the serenade although they evidently were enjoying it immensely.

"Close the door behind you, Virgillia," advised Rosalia in her sweetest company tone, "so the children will not awaken." All eyes turned to Virgillia. Francesco introduced her to the guests.

"Let's drink a toast to Virgillia," shouted Luigi. Salvatore gladly took another glass of wine. Francesco drew a cool, sparkling bottle of wine from the water filled washtub. Rosalia passed the cheesecakes for the company.

Virgillia now knew the reason why ma made the cheesecakes and why Rosalia kept the secret from her. Her serenade was to be a surprise, which indeed it was. Virgillia felt Signora Longobardo's eyes on her. Signora Longobardo smiled at Virgillia and patted the empty chair beside her. Virgillia seated herself. Ma passed the plate with the cheesecakes and after Signora Longobardo agreed that they were the most delicious cheesecakes she had ever eaten, she asked Virgillia the type of work she did and where she had received her training. Virgillia liked her pleasant voice. She spoke English well with a slight Italian accent.

"We don't often come to New York, although we originally settled in Manhattan when we came from Italy. It seems a hundred years ago. We should try to come more often and meet more of our countrymen, especially those who come from our village as the Vinas did."

She is only trying to make conversation to be civil, thought Virgillia.

The music had ceased. Francesco kept filling the wine glasses, just as they did after a serenade in Italy.

"You allow your only son to live away from home, Signora Longobardo?" Francesco asked, his forehead furrowing with disapproval.

Signora Longobardo smiled at Francesco's question, while her husband answered.

"What can my son do on a farm, Francesco. He is a college graduate with several degrees. He must make his own way in the world. If you had a son, would you shelter him as you would a girl, then try to marry him off?" Francesco winced. He felt uncomfortable. He did not like the way Signore Longobardo laughed hilariously and slapped his shoulder. He thought Virgillia would have to pass the test of acceptance with the Longobardos, but it seemed as though he was up for trial. Francesco turned the conversation to other channels.

"Are you and Signora Longobardo coming to the Festa Della Madonna Della Civita social in July?" asked Francesco pointing to the picture of the Madonna in whose honor the feast was celebrated. Signora Longobardo crossed herself and threw the Madonna a kiss.

"Santissima Madonna," she whispered devoutly.

"This year we'll try to come," promised Signore Longobardo.

"Will you invite your son?" asked Luigi eagerly.

"Our son is a busy man Luigi. He may not have the time to come to the Festa," he said slowly.

"Perhaps I can coax him to attend." Signora Longobardo nodded her head convincingly as she smiled on the company.

Maria and Rosalia exchanged broad grins. Perhaps Virgillia would meet her prospective suitor at the social.

The wine was going fast and Rosalia could see that Giuseppe seemed worried because they had not had the pleasure of meeting Virgillia's suitor, but she would tell Giuseppe that trying to get Virgillia married was worth a whole barrel of wine. Giuseppe now fished for another bottle of wine from the washtub. Francesco was annoyed with Luigi and Salvatore. The Longobardos were vague about their own son. He didn't even live at home. He took the bottle from Giuseppe's hand. Francesco felt as though he had stepped into mud and was stuck fast. However, he had to make the best of a bad bargain and changed to a gayer mood. The company was present. They had serenaded Virgillia and he had brought the wine from the cellar for the purpose of celebration.

"Let's drink to youth and romance," he said gayly. The wine was slowly having its effect on Francesco. He swung the bottle over his head. It hit the wall and it splattered on the floor. For a second, silence reigned then Luigi burst into song.

"It's a sign of feasting, a sign of feasting," shouted Rosalia excitedly. Salvatore licked his lips as he stared at the red pool forming at his feet. Another bottle came to the rescue.

"It is a sign of feasting," agreed Francesco, trying to believe his own words.

Signora Derella had helped the serenaders sing "O Virgie, O Virgie." She had joined in the laughter and conversation, then she had gone to her own flat, because she had a headache. Now she returned just as the bottle broke on the wall. She walked slowly around the kitchen, her arms folded on her chest. The glimmer of the wine splattered on the floor aroused her superstitious faith.

"When a wine bottle breaks on the wall," she said ominously, "it is not a sign of feasting but of misfortune."

It was three o'clock in the morning when the guests left the Vina flat, and Virgillia found her way to bed again.

Virgillia liked the Longobardos. Ma and pa had been disappointed. The Longobardos had made them feel a bit foolish and had promised them nothing. They had a son who lived his own life. How could they choose a wife for him? How the Longobardos had laughed at Signora Derella's words about the broken wine bottle. Signora Derella didn't like the Longobardos.

The only bad luck, Mr. Longobardo had said, was that the bottle had broken and the wine had spilled on the floor—what a waste.

It seemed the Vinas had been discussing the serenade all night. When Virgillia awoke the next morning after her few hours of restless sleep, she heard Giuseppe's quiet, kind voice from the kitchen. "Rosalia, we'll need more money to make new wine, if Virgie marries within the year. I'll have to open the shoe shine parlor at six o'clock every morning."

"I don't know what's wrong with Luigi and Salvatore. Instead of bringing the lover they bring the parents of the lover," Rosalia said irritably.

"Rosalia is right," Maria plodded around the kitchen, setting the breakfast dishes on the kitchen table. "Their son doesn't even live at home. He may not be the marrying kind." Her voice was edged with disappointment.

"I agree with all of you," announced Francesco forlornly, "but even if he had come, what would a wordly man see in a scatterbrained girl like Virgillia?"

"Pa, but we did have a good time, didn't we?" laughed Rosalia.

Maria grinned too, remembering Virgillia's serenade. They did have a wonderful time. The serenade took Maria back to Italy and her youthful romance with Francesco.

"The missionary priest said every thing is up to God. We must all conform to God's will," reasoned Maria aloud. "Not only the easy things come from God, but also the difficult problems like wanting to get Virgillia married to a good man like Giuseppe or Ferdinando."

"But we must still use our talents to the best of our abilities, Maria, and that is what we are doing. Of course what is to be is written," Francesco finished lamely.

The postman's shrill whistle sounded from the ground floor.

"Francesco Vina—Fran—ces—co—Vi—na!"

The Vinas got excited whenever the postman trilled their name up and down the dingy hallways while the children scuttled downstairs for the mail. Their feeling of importance grew as they thought of their neighbors wondering at the contents of their correspondence.

Virgillia slipped into a flowered kimono that Rosalia had sewed for her and ran downstairs in her slippered feet. The children were still soundly asleep. The letter was addressed to Francesco Vina in Luisa's awkward scrawl. Virgillia gave pa the envelope and waited with bated breath for Luisa's reply to her invitation to visit the family while ma went to Cousin Marietta. Pa looked at the envelope from all angles before the light from the window while everyone waited impatiently for the news within.

"Franci, can't you see it's an envelope?" Maria drawled. She knew of Francesco's inability to read. She was also anxious to know if Luisa would stay with the children.

"Take it, Rosalia, and see what Luisa says. I thought it was written in Italian." When a letter arrived from Italy written in Italian, he would say the writing was a scrawl and he couldn't read it.

Dear Family,

"Hmmmm—how sweet she begins." Rosalia always gave her desired or undesired opinion when she read a letter.

I'm so happy that ma is making a trip to Cousin Marietta. I hope it will be a boy this time. Ferdinando is working in Connecticut right now. They are building one family houses and he is setting the windows. It would be nice for me to visit. I'm all tired out and would like a change to iron out my nerves.

Love,
Luisa

Luisa should know better than to iron out her nerves in the Vina menage, thought Virgillia, as she quickly dressed for her halfday at the office. It had been a hectic week for Virgillia as a dishevelled Rosalia hurled orders and advice on how she and Luisa should best manage the family while she, ma, and pa were away. The weeks had just flown after Easter. It was the beginning of June now and Rosalia had completely forgotten the dresses that had to be sewed for the children for the Festa Della Madonna Della Civita social, which arrived on July twenty-first. It was an unusually brilliant feast day for the children. The Italiam immigrants wanted to impress each other with their new found security in a new land which was gauged by the way the children dressed. New dresses and new shoes were a must. It was the month of the year that drained the meager savings the Vinas may have managed to save, but to honor their Madonna, it was ungrudgingly spent even though they spent the money to give their egos a lift.

"The children can wear their Sunday dresses this year," suggested Virgillia, hoping Rosalia would agree so that she and Luisa would not be burdened with the problem of sewing for them but Francesco and Maria looked up in alarm.

"The children wore those dresses last year," stated Francesco disapprovingly.

"We offer fresh flowers to the Madonna and new dresses make the children look like flowers," said Maria smiling at the Madonna.

"It will also show our friends that we are doing well, Virgillia," said Rosalia. Maria and Francesco nodded proudly, and Virgillia cringed inwardly as she looked at the yards and yards of gingham and percale piled on the machine, rising like a mountain, to honor the Madonna.

"Let the children tell you the styles they want so that they'll look happy on that day. Luisa took up designing and pattern making at the evening trade school before she married. She knows how to cut patterns from newspapers to fit the different children. Don't cut the material first. Remember, first cut the newspaper patterns." Virgillia steeled herself for the ordeal of sewing for the little sisters who were never satisfied.

She liked sewing dainty, frilly things like tea aprons. She didn't like mass production. She knew satisfying the capricious children would not be easy, but Luisa was a good dressmaker. That is why she felt relieved when she heard that Luisa was willing bait.

"And don't forget when the children come from school, see that they take off their shoes. After all they were only bought for Easter and if they are careful, with a little polish, the shoes will look like new on the feast day." Rosalia's lips were moist for hours at a time, as she talked and talked and bustled around with her own importance.

"Let the children play in the parlor or the second bedroom but be careful of the furniture." Virgillia was glad that Rosalia's orders demanded no replies.

Virgillia hastened home after her morning at the office. A desolate office with Donald still in Boston.

She passed the church of the Holy Redeemer and thought she would step in and spend a few moments in the empty church. She loved the stillness she felt within its walls, the stillness that evaded the Vina flat at all times. She sat in the last pew and felt immediately relaxed and at peace. Father Ignatius lighting a candle on the main altar saw her. Slowly he came up the aisle to greet her. He had been her Sunday school teacher all through the elementary grades.

"How are you, Virgillia? How is the family?" Suddenly she felt limp within herself. Why should she lie to Father Ignatius and tell him she was fine and so was the family. Her frustration rebelled, fizzed, and bubbled over.

"Ma is having another baby, Father Ignatius. I wish ma would stop having babies. We are seven children now. We are overcrowded. I work hard and must turn in my entire salary. Rosalia has her own family and she must help ma. Now she is minding my business, helping pa find me a husband."

Good Father Ignatius was quite taken aback by Virgillia's

resentment of her family's problems. He had known Virgillia as a quiet, almost withdrawn person with a good memory for remembering her catechism questions and answers. Now he understood Francesco's problem with Virgillia. She was ready to overthrow any system that did not suit her at the moment. He would say a special prayer at mass for Francesco that he and Rosalia would find a suitable suitor for Virgillia. Francesco and Maria had problems enough without a young, rebellious daughter.

He now smiled at Virgillia and sat beside her.

"Virgillia, Italy has been an improvident mother and her hungry children have come to America, whose land has been blessed with natural resources. America adopts all hungry sons and daughters of other countries, giving all a chance to work, to better themselves, to live more comfortably. Your parents are doing the best they can. Sometimes it takes several generations in America for an easier life. Of course, you, as part of an immigrant family, must help financially, if you are able. When you marry and have daughters of your own, you will not fear America because you are born here and your daughters will meet their own husbands. Don't be too harsh, Virgillia. Your parents left loved ones and the land they loved to give you and your sisters a better life. To them, no matter how it may seem to you, it is a better life, or they would have returned to Italy."

"But why must ma keep having children, if it isn't easy to support them," insisted Virgillia.

"This is your mother's life, Virgillia. You will have your own life to worry about, as you grow older."

Virgillia looked glumly at her hands. She would have felt better sitting a few moments by herself. Father Ignatius had not helped her and now she felt like a fool, rebelling against her lot in the Vina flat.

He patted her hand gently and arose saying, "Virgillia, lascio corre il mondo e ride sempre." She understood the meaning of the Italian proverb, "Let the world glide and laugh always." Now she looked up at his gentle face and did his bidding. She smiled. She felt better. After all he understood the futility of her rebellion. Father Ignatius quietly returned to the altar and Virgillia hurried home.

Maria was sprawled in her favorite seat near the window. Spring was hastening into summer and its heat was making itself felt early. Maria was pale. Virgillia saw the worried expression on pa's face as he prepared an orange drink for ma, breaking a piece of ice from the large chunk in the ice box, slipping it into a glass. He squeezed an orange and poured the juice in the glass. His fear of losing Maria was transmitted to Virgillia. She now looked beseechingly at the Madonna.

"Spare ma for us," Virgillia silently prayed.

Pa stared impatiently at the much embroidered clock on the mantlepiece.

"When is Luisa coming?" he asked the question aloud to no one in particular. No one was like Rosalia, thought Francesco, sharp, capable, clocklike. Virgillia suddenly heard a loud honking taxi horn. Rosalia hastened upstairs, her face flushed, saying, "Luisa is waiting in the taxi. Ferdinando spoiled Luisa. She rides in taxis and is always stylishly dressed." Rosalia jealously spoke her mind as she helped ma slip into her best, black dress, then clamped a hat on her own head, making sure that the strands of flying hair were well tucked under the brim. Looking at the yards and yards of material on the sewing machine appeased a bit of the envy she felt for Luisa, who living away from the Vina family seemed to have an easier life. She'll have a chance to forget her fancy self, taking care of ma's family for a few weeks, thought Rosalia with malicious satisfaction.

Francesco ran noisily downstairs. He wished the tenants would see the taxi before it drove away. He wanted the tenants to see that Luisa had married well. He cupped his hands to his mouth and called Rosalia loudly from the second floor.

"Let Virgillia come and help with the children, Rosalia."

"Sure, even pa spoils her," she said to herself, then she thought of pa's pride in her when they had discussed rich men marrying girls like Virgillia. She felt ashamed of herself for a moment. After all, God had given her the strength of mind and body to manage her home and Giuseppe's shoe shine parlor well, and she still had the energy to help ma. She loved all the management that came under her control. Pa would see the difference after he returned home with Luisa and Virgillia at the helm. He would be still prouder of her capabilities, she told herself.

"Hurry, ma, before the children begin to cry," now whispered Rosalia looking at Caterina and Angie's drooping lips.

Maria stood for a long, wistful moment looking over her brood, then she smiled tenderly, stooped and kissed the children.

"Be good, children." Virgillia ascending the stairs with one of Luisa's small grips dropped it and flung her arms around her mother. Maria's fleshy face rested for a moment on Virgillia's strong, firm cheek.

"Take care of one another," whispered Maria. Virgillia felt a lump in her throat. The flat would feel so empty without good, placid ma.

Luisa was sitting in the taxi when Rosalia and Maria reached the street. A slight crease of impatience lined her forehead. Rosalia had to admit that Luisa and her round-faced children dressed all in white appeared prosperous.

"Ah, Luisa, Luisa, the children don't even know their own grandfather." Francesco proudly drew the children out of the taxi. The Vina family excused Luisa for not visiting often because she traveled with her carpenter husband as he went from job to job. Rosalia welcomed Luisa with a smile on her lips and an annoyed expression of haste lining her forehead.

The tenants had come downstairs and crowded around the taxi giving Luisa and her children a glad welcome. Luisa pressed a five-dollar bill in the taxi driver's hand, giving him Cousin Marietta's address. Amid the well wishes of the laughing, jabbering tenants, Maria, Francesco, and Rosalia drove away.

"Make it a boy this time," yelled the neighbors in high glee.

After ma, pa, and Rosalia left, Virgillia and Luisa felt strange for a while. They had not seen each other in two years.

"You've changed, Luisa," said Virgillia as she quickly took off her office dress and slipped into a housedress. Luisa's black hair was set in waves away from her face. Her thick glasses seemed finer without frames. Virgillia liked her white tailored suit.

Luisa had a peculiar face, thought Virgillia, as though she was seeing her for the first time. Her eyes were large with the same uncertain shape as her face. They were pretty black eyes, but the left one would draw at times. Luisa often rolled them to strengthen the nerve as the eye doctor had advised. She was now rolling her eyes as she spoke.

"Virgillia, I have traveled around so much with Ferdinando in the past two years that I almost forgot how horrible this section is." Luisa crinkled the sides of her nose. "The smell of those garbage cans, ugh." Virgillia laughed.

"You'll get used to them all over again, Luisa," Virgillia said cheerfully, then added as an afterthought, "you won't think of the garbage cans downstairs when you smell pa's basil and mint plants on the fire escape. They sweeten the air."

Luisa looked approvingly at Virgillia as Virgillia scampered around the room righting the scattered articles that had been hurriedly left about. The children remained downstairs with Luisa's children, while the neighbors chatted with the newcomers. It was always a surprise to the neighbors when a girl, raised in their tenement, married and returned with her children. They felt as though the children had a special place in their affections. Virgillia had grown graceful and pretty, thought Luisa.

"Is pa still very strict, Virgillia?" smiled Luisa.

"He's downright impossible, Luisa. Pa is trying to get Luigi and Salvatore to find me a husband the way they matched you and Rosalia."

Luisa giggled, then laughed aloud.

"We didn't do so bad, Virgillia. I fell in love with Ferdinando the moment I saw him and Rosalia seems well suited to Giuseppe."

Virgillia looked squarely at Luisa.

"Luisa, I have already fallen in love!" Luisa's mouth fell open.

"Does the family know? Where did you meet him? Has he proposed?" All the questions seemed to fall at once from Luisa's lips.

"I met him in the office. I'm his secretary. No, I haven't told the family because I don't know a thing about him. He hasn't dated me, although I've been out to lunch with him."

Luisa bit her lips. She felt misgivings. She had come to look after ma's family, thinking her sisters were still young and immature. She had not expected to find Virgillia, the young lady she had become with a decided mind of her own. By Sunday evening, Virgillia knew that Luisa realized the responsibility of caring for the Vina family was a tremendous task, even though they had laughed all day, as Virgillia filled in the details of the serenade and the family's reaction to Luigi and Salvatore for bringing the parents of the suitor instead of the suitor. They even giggled over ma's self imposed task of converting Signora Derella to a good Christian, while she tenaciously held onto the faith in the horns that were going to bring Virgillia a husband.

"I don't understand why ma and pa don't wait until I decide on marriage for myself," said Virgillia thoughtfully.

"Pa is only trying to make life easier for you by introducing you to a worthwhile suitor," Luisa advised gently.

"Pa is trying too hard," frowned Virgillia. "I suppose you're right," she added as an afterthought.

Virgillia had to admit that Luisa was pleasant company. She sighed. Saturday afternoon dragged, there was Sunday, and then Monday and the office. Would Donald be in Boston?

THIRTEEN

Virgillia felt a glad lift to her heart, on Monday morning, when she entered the office and found Donald sitting at her desk. He was there. She was glad.

"I've been on a merry-go-round," he exclaimed, grinning at her.

"I'm looking for these cards." He handed Virgillia a list of names as he arose. His fingers brushed against her cool hand.

"Nice to have you back," she said.

"This morning I feel as though I'm sitting on top of the world." His eyes held her inquiring glance.

"I'm glad you feel so chipper," she said, then thought, has he entertained Meg on the weekend that he feels so good? She felt a twinge of jealousy.

"The world is a grand place," she added without enthusiasm.

"Would you like to take a trip with me around the world, Virgillia." he asked eagerly. Virgillia glanced at him quizzically. Donald certainly was in fine feather. She wondered now if he had had a few highballs with Ben Worth before coming to the office.

"Wouldn't you like to come with me?" he asked again.

"If wishes were wings, beggars would fly," quoted Virgillia from the nursery rhyme. "You must be dreaming, Donald."

"Let's make the dream come true." His eyes shone mischievously. Virgillia now stared at him.

"We can travel around the world in New York, you know," he said eagerly.

"Oh, Donald," she laughed, "for a while I didn't know

what had happened to you."

"Last week was hectic. I was too busy to have a decent lunch. We'll start our travels this afternoon." His mother expected to stay another week at his apartment. He had no alternative but to take her to lunch. Even when Ben Worth told Donald's mother that he had given Donald a beautiful secretary, his mother smiled indulgently.

"I'll be the interlude between his old and new love," she had said complacently.

His mother came so seldom to the city that Donald felt he had to sacrifice his time for her. She had asked Ben Worth, "Is she dark or light?"

"She is the most beautiful brunette with olive cheeks and limpid black eyes." His mother had scoffed.

"Donald is partial to blondes."

"But blackheads get under your skin," Ben had countered laughing.

How right he was, thought Donald. He glanced at Virgillia's fingers. She wore no rings. She must still be free of heart, he thought, relieved.

After all the hectic hours spent at home since Donald had left for Boston, being invited to lunch was recompense indeed, thought Virgillia. Pa was right, he always said you can't have joy without a bit of pain. Right now she forgot the pain of his absence. She only felt joy.

Donald had invited her to see the world with him in New York. It was an exciting invitation.

The lunch hour that Virgillia spent with Donald was indeed fascinating. The taxi spun its way down Fifth Avenue, south of Washington Square, straight into the heart of Greenwich Village. Although Virgillia had been born in the city of New York, she was a stranger to its interesting haunts. She was now captivated by the winding streets of the village, ending abruptly or losing themselves only to be caught again, several blocks away. The mellowed bricks of the gracious homes built with long windows and massive doors standing proudly before well cared for flower gardens charmed Virgillia. She was so near and yet so far from the slum area, on the lower east side where she lived.

"How quaint," she whispered.

"The Sapokanikan used to be here," said Donald. He liked to feel Virgillia's soft black eyes looking at him questioningly.

"The Sapokanikan was an old Indian Village," he informed her.

"Just imagine the Indians marching through the lanes coming through the woods along Broadway carrying game to their squaws," she marvelled.

"I bring my squaw to the game." They giggled as the taxi stopped before a restaurant with a huge sign painted in orange and black. Huge letters glared in green, "Pirate's Den." Once inside its darkened interior Virgillia had to shut her eyes, which stung from the glare of the sun outside. When her eyes got accustomed to the dim light, she was surprised by the waiters who were dressed as pirates, with the most grotesque painted faces. The restaurant was patterned after a pirate ship. Young men with long hair and flowing neckties, young girls with saucy lips, smocked and with paint from their pallettes staining their fingers, joked, kissed, and danced with gay abandon. Virgillia watched the scene with avid interest.

"The real artists are usually too busy to play. Some people play at art," remarked Donald.

The unusual atmosphere of the restaurant transformed into a huge pirate ship held Virgillia spellbound.

"I almost smell the tang of the salty air." Donald unfolded his napkin which had a ragged edge, then playfully held on to the edge of the table, while he swayed from side to side, as though he was on a moving ship.

"I feel almost seasick," he joked. They laughed like two

children playing a delightful game.

"Do they serve seafood?" Virgillia looked over the menu, which was printed on a paper resembling a piece of driftwood.

"The pirates wouldn't give a damsel only seafood. Caviar and chicken for my sweetheart." Donald brought his hand down on the table. The glasses tinkled merrily. Virgillia blushed. Was Donald talking for the pirates or for himself?

It was fun picking at the chicken salad which Virgillia ordered.

"I almost feel like a pirate with all this atmosphere." Donald's eyes twinkled when at the end of their lunch, they swung to the throbbing strains of bewitching music.

"I like you in any role, Donald," Virgillia said softly.

"In a frankfurter roll too?" he teased. Virgillia looked at her wristwatch and tugged Donald's sleeve.

"Time is up, Pirate Long," she laughed.

The sun shone across the quaint winding streets and stately homes, giving them a soft splendor as the taxi raced back to the office. The sun splashed on Virgillia's bright red bolero, making it resplendent, as resplendent as their charmed smiles. Their youthful exuberance, long held in check by study, disappointments, and rigid discipline, once set in motion came bubbling to the surface, each delighted at the eager joy they felt in mutual companionship.

The taxi raced underneath the arch at Washington Square.

"This used to be Potter's Field and the public gallows a hundred years ago." She felt a shadow on her gay mood. It would be wonderful to have Donald always at her side. He had only asked her to lunch because last week he had had a hectic week. He wanted to relax and she was as good as any other girl with whom to have lunch, she thought dismally.

When they returned to the office, it seemed as though hell had broken loose. A prospective customer had appeared unexpectedly. He wanted plans for a large boarding house and he had to have them at once. The way the tall, nervous man acted you would think he wanted Donald to take them out of the air, defended Virgillia.

She expected Donald to be busy for the remainder of the week but was happily surprised the next day when Donald buzzed her asking her to lunch again.

"Today we'll go to Spain," announced Donald as they rode toward the Spanish quarters at Twenty-third Street and Seventh Avenue. It was cooler today. Donald threw a red plaid blanket over her knees. Virgillia smiled gratefully.

"I don't see any signs of Spain?" Virgillia looked up and down the street.

"Did you expect to see a bullfight?" smiled Donald. "Spaniards are reticent. They don't display themselves outwardly." The taxi driver had been told to drive to Casa Blanca. Virgillia spotted the large white sign before the canopied restaurant. Dona Blanca knew Donald well. She was pleased to see him with a new girl friend. As she led them to her private quarters, she insisted that Virgillia looked like a Spanish senorita with her warm, dark coloring and red lips. Meg was different from Virgillia, she was telling Donald. Meg was cool and light like the dawn. Virgillia was more like the flaming sun, setting on a hot day. Virgillia felt numb. Dona Blanca seemed to know Meg very well. Now Virgillia remembered the Valentine card, from Meg to Donald. She sensed that Donald felt uncomfortable as Dona Bianca compared her to Meg. She invited Donald and Virgillia to make themselves comfortable on her Spanish-styled sofa, covered with gay mantillas.

Dona Blanca was dressed in native Spanish costume. She tucked a red rose on a comb on a black, silk shawl, and thrust it on her highly coiffured hair. Her large proportions moved rhythmically to and fro as she brought forward her store of rich delicacies and old vintage wine. They had a lunch of tortillas, hot and delicious. Dona Blanca's dark eyes sparkled happily as she served her guests, her lips opened to the size of an egg when she smiled. She listened breathlessly to Donald's bit of gossip concerning the people they both knew who frequented Casa Blanca. Virgillia walked to an alcove to admire a variety of Spanish souvenirs, when she heard Dona Blanca ask Donald in a loud whisper, "Whatever happened to Meg? Surely I thought you would be married to her by this time." Virgillia felt rooted to the spot. The phone rang and she never heard Donald's answer. Virgillia wondered if she had heard right. Donald was looking at her adoringly. She knew so little about his private life. She wondered.

"Bah!" uttered Dona Blanca in disgust when she returned from her phone call. "Why must the telephone ring while my friends are visiting?" She called some strange names in a melodious voice and immediately two young men with guitars and a tall, graceful girl came into the room. Instantly strains of Spanish music filled the air. The girl clicked her castenets and danced to the sweet refrain. Dona Blanca contributed her throaty voice to the melody. Donald squeezed Virgillia's hand. With the exception of that cold, awful moment when she stood in the alcove and heard Dona Blanca asking Donald whatever had happen to Meg, Virgillia brought away happy thoughts of the Spanish quarter.

FOURTEEN

Monday evening Virgillia kept the stars in her eyes when she returned home from the office, even though Luisa looked annoyed and said that the day was fraught with unholy clamor. During Saturday and Sunday Luisa's chidren had held themselves aloof from their young cousins. When they finally did warm up to each other, battles raged. It was adding salt to Giuseppe's wounds, not having capable Rosalia at home with his children. Being a quiet, peace-loving fellow, he confided his problem to Virgillia, telling her how Luisa always thought her children were in the right. He swallowed his hurt and promised to take Nicky and Nanny to the shoe shine parlor, returning with them at noon and in the evening, but Virgillia remonstrated with him, telling him that that would cause a rift in Luisa's relationship to him. Virgillia, sorry for Giuseppe's plight, won the children to peace with candy kisses and lollypops that evening.

The bumpy sofa did much to cement the friendship of the young cousins. It bumped up and down pleasantly. A count of ten was allowed each in turn. Luisa and Virgillia cutting paper patterns on the kitchen table the following evenings were satisfied to hear the children's gurgling laughter, being too busy to explore the extent of the damage to the sofa.

Luisa was very much interested in Virgillia's romance with Donald. Virgillia described all the places of interest where she lunched.

"When Donald suggested seeing the world in New York, Luisa, I never dreamed there are so many quaint and interesting places on Manhattan Island."

"It's true," agreed Luisa. "People born and bred in New York sometimes know so little about their own wonderful city." Then she became pensive.

"Virgillia, do you think Donald could be in love with you? If he would propose to you before ma and pa came home, perhaps you can introduce him to the family, then pa, ma, and Rosalia will forget about the suitor whom Luigi and Salvatore are trying to find for you."

"I wish I could make him fall in love with me," Virgillia clasped her hands prayerfully, then she thought of Dona Blanca's words, "Whatever happened to Meg. I surely thought you would be married by this time."

"Luisa, what if he is in love with this Meg and is only having lunch with me to pass the time of day?"

Luisa laid down her scissors and looked thoughtfully at Virgillia.

"It could be. You might only be building castles in the air. Virgillia, this can't go on. You've got to take the bull by the horns and know exactly where you stand. At this rate, you'll become an emotional volcano. And you know what happens when a volcano erupts, Virgillia? Why don't you invite Donald here for dinner?"

Virgillia looked aghast.

"But—but, Luisa. He lives on Central Park West. How can I invite him here, the East Side slums, the melting pot!" Virgillia made a depressing gesture with her two hands.

"Virgillia, Donald must see you in your own setting and see you as you are," Luisa advised wisely.

"Luisa, what if he should come here and I should lose him entirely?" There was anguish in Virgillia's plea.

Luisa felt sorry for Virgillia.

"You can't go on like this forever, Virgillia. Isn't it best if you know definitely how he feels about you? If he is not in love with you, then you can forget him and perhaps you will welcome Luigi and Salvatore with their prospective suitor for you." Luisa spoke slowly. Virgillia had to admit her advice was sensible, sound, but, oh, so hard to take. Like medicine, it was bitter but good for you.

The following afternoon at the office, Donald buzzed Virgillia.

"May we continue our travels?" he asked.

Donald was pleased to hear, "I'll go anywhere with you, Donald." Next week he would be free to invite Virgillia to see one of the operettas she liked. This time he would not go on her free pass. He smiled, amused at his unusual romance with Virgillia. From his end it was a romance. He hoped she felt the same way. He was confident because she always was eager to go with him.

Virgillia took off her tomato-colored large brimmed felt hat and rested her curly head on his shoulder in the taxi. She unbuttoned her white woolen coat which she wore over a white linen dress, which Luis had generously loaned her.

They rode uptown to Harlem. The Negro policeman on the corner was tap dancing. Children played merrily on the streets and some young fellows in high hats and spats were harmonizing on the street corner.

"They must be theatrical folks," said Donald looking at his wristwatch.

"It's twelve-thirty and you must be starved, Virgillia." He told the taxi driver to stop before a brightly painted restaurant called THE HAVEN. A negro band played a delirious rhythm. A songstress was singing and emoting a popular tune.

"They have music in their souls," said Virgillia admiringly as they finished a delicious lunch with more turkey than they could eat. The rhythm kept everybody hopping. Unlike the Dance of the Ghetto Socialites, Virgillia didn't mind dancing with Donald.

"Tomorrow, we'll visit our Eastern friends," promised

Donald who seemed to be enjoying this tour of New York as much as Virgillia.

"Seeing the world in New York is exciting." Virgillia's eyes shone eagerly.

Although Virgillia had never been in Chinatown in New York, she knew they had arrived, on the following day, when through the taxi window she saw the narrow streets, with its structures rebuilt in pagoda style, so typically Chinese. The children with straight, black hair and slanting, brown eyes, stared squarely at intruding strangers. Virgillia imagined herself transported suddenly to the Orient.

Donald picked a souvenir with a transparent celluloid shutter on a piece of teakwood fashioned like a pagoda. Behind the shutter sat a Chinese Buddha with a long pipe. Donald gave it to Virgillia.

"I'm the little figure sitting behind the shutter, Virgillia, 'Wouldst that my heart lived within glass shutters.'" He smiled whimsically at her.

She held the souvenir tightly in her hand. She liked the subtle ways in which Donald spoke of his love for her. She would keep the souvenir on her desk and during the long hours when he would be in conference or busy behind the door marked Private, she would see Donald behind the little shutter and think of the words, "Would that my heart lived within glass shutters." She would like to change the words to "Would that our hearts, beating as one, lived within glass shutters," then let her family peek in the glass shutters to see their love.

Over the carved teakwood table in the dimly lighted Chinese restaurant, its mysterious dragons and serpents painted in flamboyant colors, Virgillia's radiance dimmed slightly. The green-eyed dragon seemed to snap at her and all because she was deciding whether to invite Donald to her home for dinner the coming Saturday. Luisa was right. She had to face reality. She had to learn more about Donald's private life and he had to know her better too. He must see her in her own environment and if he had absolutely no interest in her, he would not accept her invitation. That was the reason why the dragons painted on the walls of the restaurant were making her feel jittery. Would Donald accept her invitation?

"Just because we are in China, Virgillia, doesn't mean that you have to worship the dragons on the walls." Donald took the pagoda from her hands and set it on the table.

"Donald, I was thinking," Virgillia hesitated. Should she invite him to dinner at her home? She knew she was desperately in love with him. Could she bear to have her dream collapse if he refused to accept her invitation?

He took her two hands in his and looked at her questioningly. "I—Donald—I have enjoyed these luncheons with you Donald. Won't you have dinner with me at home Saturday afternoon?" She spoke quietly, anxious to hear his answer.

"An old bachelor would love a home cooked meal, Virgillia." He seemed delighted, thought Virgillia. Her misgivings vanished.

"I'm being silly," she thought. Again she looked at the dragons. She felt apprehensive and shuddered.

"Donald, I have had enough of China. On the street before Chinatown I saw a store filled with gypsies. Let's take a look at them before we drive back to the office," suggested Virgillia.

There seemed to be great excitement from within one of the gayly curtained store windows where the gypsies migrated for the winter and spring. Old cars of every description lined the narrow street. Women, old and young, wearing long, brightly flowered skirts, their dark, gleaming hair plaited down their shoulders, or rolled in a loose coil on their necks, their throats and wrists tinkling with all kinds of baubles and trinkets, were busily moving their belongings to the different cars lined at the curb. Donald and Virgillia joined the throng outside this particular store where there was singing and dancing. An old crone beckoned to them, asking if they wanted to have their fortunes told.

Donald shook his head negatively and pityingly placed a fifty-cent piece in her outstretched gnarled palm.

"Thank you, thank you," she whined. "I see much happiness for you. We have had so much sickness and trouble this winter that we are glad to hit the open road again. We have been waiting for Gustu's wedding. He is the chief's son." She pointed to the open door of the store. Donald and Virgillia could see the rich tapestries and thick rugs that luxuriously lined the chief's floor. Virgillia and Donald stood with the many immigrants who made their home on the lower East Side of Manhattan during the early twenties, Hungarians, Romanians, Poles, Italians, Germans, and Jews, all anxious to see a Gypsy wedding.

There was great confusion within. People were dancing, prancing, yelling, swaying to and fro, drunk with the pleasures of their own emotions. The bride gayly bedecked with jewels happily started the wedding dance. Around and around she danced, faster and faster, until exhausted she fell in the arms of the groom who did not take part in the dance. Quickly he ran through the crowd with the limp bride in his arms to his waiting ramshackle car. The guests did not seem to mind their disappearance but danced on and on, jubilantly, their shrieks of laughter echoing and re-echoing down the squalid street.

"How different from that other wedding?" Virgillia said softly.

"Which other wedding?" questioned Donald, as he took her arm and led her away from the crowd.

"Don't you remember the lovely bride we saw entering Saint Patrick's Cathedral on Fifth Avenue, when we took our first bus ride?"

"I only remember you on that bus ride." Donald did say such nice things, thought Virgillia, her eyes sparkling happily.

FIFTEEN

Now that Donald had accepted Virgillia's dinner date, Luisa and Virgillia set aside making the dresses for the children during the evenings. Instead they washed, scrubbed and scoured every corner of the four room flat, in lieu of Donald's invitation to dinner. Tommy's resentment was slowly rising. Whenever she tried to tell Virgillia the style dress she preferred for the Festa Della Madonna Della Civita social, Virgillia would shoo her away, telling her that at that particular moment it was more important to wash the kitchen windows, starch curtains, or scrub floors than to discuss styles, patterns, and dresses. Tommy could not understand what possessed Luisa and Virgillia. They were forever whispering and giggling. Tommy wondered if Luisa had convinced Virgillia to accept the suitor whom Luigi and Salvatore were trying to locate for her.

"Virgillia, I saw Luigi and Salvatore this afternoon," announced Tommy one evening, studying Virgillia's face to see if she showed interest, but Virgillia looked at Luisa and said, "Didn't you tell them that Virgillia left home?" Luisa and Virgillia laughed hilariously at that.

No, thought Tommy, puzzled more than ever. They are not preparing the flat for Luigi, Salvatore, and the suitor. On Saturday morning Luisa took Tommy marketing. Luisa bought a spring chicken, mushrooms, lettuce, peas and a strawberry shortcake.

"Be careful, Tommy, when you carry the cake. We don't want the cream to splatter all over the box. It's for special company. Virgillia's friend from the office is having dinner with her tonight. You must help keep the children quiet in Rosalia's flat while they are having dinner. Remember, he is special company."

Tommy was startled. Luisa was not working with pa, ma, and Rosalia to get Virgillia married through Luigi and Salvatore. Tommy was curious to see Virgillia's boy friend from the office. Now she knew why they had scrubbed and cleaned during the week.

After lunch Virgillia and Luisa sighed happily. The flat sparkled.

"Donald won't come until five o'clock. We can spend the afternoon basting the children's dresses," suggested Virgillia.

Tommy tried again to tell Virgillia the style pattern she wanted for her dress, but Virgillia banished her to the parlor with all the children. Tommy's resentment flamed anew with the passing moments. While Luisa and Virgillia went to ask Signora Derella how to prepare the mushrooms, Tommy quickly took all the newspaper patterns that Luisa and Virgillia had cut, put them in the iron sink and lit a match to them. In a moment the flames spread and rose to the ceiling.

"Virgie, Virgie, Virgie! Come quick!" screamed Tommy.

Virgillia never knew how Donald got there. He had felt restless with time on his hands and thought he would arrive early to get better acquainted with Virgillia's family.

"Where can I find a blanket," he shouted at Tommy.

"In there, on ma's bed," yelled Tommy excitedly, tears streaming down her cheeks.

Donald quickly threw ma's best blanket over the gray, iron sink and instantly subdued the flames that subsided entirely after a while.

The sudden terror of the fire was too much for Luisa. She gave one agonizing scream and sank to the floor. Virgillia felt her strength oozing fast but she held on to a chair as Signora Derella ran to her flat for her brandy to revive the girls.

"Roberto, Roberto, poveri figli! Rosalia should never have

left home," ranted Signora Derella.

The children who had been playing in the parlor opened the door and ran from the hall to the kitchen door. They saw Luisa on the floor and Virgillia's white frightened face staring unbelievably at Donald. With one accord they began to cry.

Signora Derella and Roberto came into the room. Roberto knelt beside Luisa and forced some brandy between her lips. Signora Derella offered Virgillia and Donald a drink. Tommy looked through fingers spread apart before her face. The fingers gave her a sort of protection against the atrocity of her act. Virgillia put her glass on the tray without touching it, but Donald pressed it to her lips. Robert wasn't reviving Luisa too well. Signora Derella took a large red polkadotted handkerchief from her pocket, soaked it with wine vinegar, and pressed it to Luisa's nose and forehead. Slowly Luisa came out of her stupor, arose, and sat limply on a chair.

Virgillia looked at the smoked wall and partly burned closet above the sink. Tommy's wild, unnatural sobs irritated her already taut nerves. She caught the curprit's shoulder and shook her fiercely.

"What made you set fire to the patterns, idiot? Answer me!"

"I didn't like the style, Virgie. Rosalia said you had to ask me if I liked it and you didn't. You wouldn't even listen to me."

"Must you burn us alive if you don't like the style, stupid?"

"Rosalia listens to me when she cuts patterns but you and Luisa are too busy talking about yourselves." Now Tommy spoke between real sobs.

Virgillia sat on the nearest chair, exasperated, placing her fingers in her ears to shut out the bedlam created by the children's cries and Signora Derella's scolding. How neatly Tommy would excuse herself to enraged Rosalia, pa, and ma, thought Virgillia, when they saw the scorched dish closet above the sink and the scorched blanket, ma's best blanket.

Virgillia turned to Donald. He had put the fire completely out in the sink, neatly rolled the blanket and placed it on Maria's bed, then turned around and met Virgillia's helpless eyes. Suddenly he smiled, then laughed heartily. This was hardly the way he had expected to meet Virgillia's family. His laughter was infectious. Virgillia smiled and felt more cheerful. She introduced him to Luisa, Roberto, and Signora Derella. After the introductions were over Signora Derella stood by the door until she caught Virgillia's eyes, then she shook her head dolefully from side to side, showing her disapproval of Virgillia entertaining men folk when Francesco, Maria, and Rosalia were not at home.

Tommy, delighted at the cheerful turn Donald's laughter brought to the little group, caught his hand and drew him toward the parlor. The children crowded around him and pushed him on the bumpy sofa.

"This is how we play," said Tommy. "I count one, two, three, four, five, six, seven, eight, nine, ten. Everytime I say an even number you must bump down on the sofa. If you miss, you're out." On the third count Donald found himself out of the game because he bumped up on an even number instead of bumping down.

"You better keep score," said Tommy pressing a paper and pencil in his hand, "so I can get a couple of turns on the sofa." When Tommy heard Virgillia's footsteps approaching, she cautioned the children and Donald not to move. "Virgillia won't want us to jump on the sofa," whispered Tommy. Donald sat on one of the spiked chairs which Rosalia had purchased for the Vina suitors and grinned at Virgillia.

"I'm sorry you came at the wrong moment, Donald," she wiped away the beads of perspiration from her forehead with her lace-trimmed handkerchief. "Ma, pa, and my oldest sister will be away for several weeks. My sister Luisa came from the Bronx with her three chidren to help me keep house."

"It's a big job, Virgillia. I'll baby-sit while you and Luisa are busy in the kitchen."

Virgillia smiled gratefully.

On her way back to the kitchen she found Signora Derella with the look of disapproval still on her face.

"I think the missionary priest is right. Cow's horns are works of the devil. They are bringing you the wrong sweetheart, Virgillia."

Signora Derella hammered a nail underneath the picture of the Madonna and hung up her horns. "I'll give them to you, dear Madonna, so you'll know I'm not using them anymore." Signora Derella piously crossed herself and clattered out of the kitchen. Virgillia looked at Luisa in astonishment. She reached for the horns but Luisa restrained her.

"Please, Virgillia, we've done enough damage since ma left with pa and Rosalia. We have almost burned the kitchen, scorched ma's best blanket, and ruined the closet above the sink. I know by this time the children must have broken the springs in the sofa. Now are we going to upset Signora Derella and lose Roberto? Leave the horns where she put them."

"What will Donald think when he sees a pair of cow's horns hanging near the picture of the Madonna?" asked Virgillia impatiently.

"We'll make him sit with his back to the horns, Virgillia. Please, Virgillia, listen to me," pleaded Luisa, still pale from her fright of the fire. Virgillia acquiesced with mixed emotions.

Donald had to admit to himself that Virgillia probably never spent a dull moment with her many sisters and Signora Derella.

He enjoyed Tommy's management of the little brood of rosy-faced, bright-eyed children. Everytime they laughed, their laughter was so infectious that he laughed too.

Virgillia now wrapped herself in her mother's large blue and white striped apron, washed the chicken, cleaned the mushrooms, and prepared the peas. She would make the salad last.

Luisa set the table. While they were busily working Signora Derella quietly walked in the kitchen. She made herself comfortable on a kitchen chair.

"Congratulations, Virgillia. Your boy friend is nice. Does pa know him?" she questioned curiously.

"I'll tell him all about my boy friend when pa comes home," Virgillia said shortly.

Luisa wished she was back in her own apartment in the Bronx. Why should she discourage Virgillia from seeing Donald, if she loved him. No one could command love. You found love in the strangest places. If Maria and Francesco had remained in Italy and if Virgillia had been born in Italy, Francesco would know that love was a happening under an olive tree, near a lake or just a walk down the street. It was natural for Francesco to feel fearful in a land with mixed races and religions, but it was difficult for Virgillia, who found herself in the marketplace, to fall in love with a man of pa's background.

Signora Derella was much concerned with this strange man who came to visit while Francesco, Maria, and Rosalia were away. She shook her head dolefully. Away from Francesco's watchful eye even Luisa had become too Americanized to allow Virgillia to entertain a strange man in their apartment. Roberto stood in the kitchen just when Tommy came to get a drink of water.

"If you don't tell pa about the fire, Signora Derella, I'll tell you where Bettina goes at night." Tommy looked impishly at Virgillia and Luisa.

"I already know where she goes, Tommy. Roberto told me." Suddenly the door opened and Bettina came into the room. She stared lamely from Signora Derella to Roberto. She knew Signora Derella would now begin to cross examine her, but with her next words Signora Derella surprised everyone.

"Bettina, Roberto told me that you work on the night shift in the five and ten cents store. Don't ever be sneaky, Bettina. Honesty is the best policy, because when you're honest, you have nothing to hide and your mind is free, free as air." Signora Derella laughed in her high cackling voice, then arose and did a few steps of the Italian dance, La Tarantella. Everyone giggled and as she left, still dancing, Roberto's eyes bore a shining happiness.

"Ma is getting well. Ma felt alone when pa died. Her mind almost snapped, but when Ma Vina took her to the mission, she didn't feel alone anymore because the missionary priest told of the wonderful saints, and the Madonna and our Lord Jesus who are all praying for us and loving us, giving us grace not to do wrong, so we won't hurt God," finished Roberto solemnly, trying to remember his mother's exact words.

"You sound like a missionary priest yourself, Roberto," laughed Luisa.

"The way Signora Derella danced right out of the kitchen, she must feel like a cherubim," giggled Virgillia, glad in knowing that ma would be pleased to hear of Signora Derella's complete conversion. Now that Signora Derella knew she had friends in heaven and on earth she wasn't angry with herself anymore, thought Virgillia, smiling.

Bettina's face glowed happily as she looked after Signora Derella's dancing figure.

This was Bettina's evening off and Virgillia included her and Roberto in her dinner party. After she introduced Bettina to Donald, Bettina whispered, "Virgillia, he is handsome."

Roberto liked Donald. They fell into an easy conversation, which was disturbed by the children's arguments. They had tired of playing on the bumpy sofa.

Roberto now clicked his fingers, and the children fell in line.

They liked Roberto's military drill and marching around

and around the parlor table. They especially liked the salute to Roberto's imaginary flag. They paraded, fell in a heap, and laughed until Signora Derella took them into her flat where she had prepared an unexpected supper for the children.

"My goodness, she has changed," Virgillia whispered to Luisa, amazed at Signora Derella's transformation.

Donald visiting her at home was a delightful experience for Virgillia. He seemed to enjoy her family of assorted sisters. He liked Roberto and openly admired blonde, pretty Bettina. He approved of the Vina teamwork, Luisa coming with her three children to help Virgillia with the housework and management of the large household. He even seemed to like Signora Derella with her piercing black eyes and her interest in the Vina affairs, although they seemed to resent her intrusion.

The meal was delicious. Donald was seated with his back to the horns. There was much laughter over the funny stories Roberto and Donald exchanged. After supper, Signora Derella had brought the children to Rosalia's flat and put the younger ones to bed. Everything went well until Donald remembered that he had left the hood of his car down. It had begun to rain. Big drops of water slapped against the windows. Virgillia had opened the game of Monopoly, which Donald said he would like to play, but he excused himself for a few minutes as he went to the street to raise the hood of his car. Going down the gaslit corridors he met Tommy.

"Signora Derella is treating the kids to ice cream." Tommy opened her palm and showed Donald a handful of nickels and dimes.

"You deserve ice cream. You've been good children," said Donald smiling.

Tommy stood looking at Donald for a long moment, then she beckoned to him. He lowered his ear to Tommy's lips. She whispered for a long time. When Donald straightened himself, the smile had left his face. He seemed stunned, tense.

Tommy scampered to the door leading to the street.

"Tommy!" called Donald, looking at his wristwatch. "Will you please tell Virgillia that I forgot a nine o'clock appointment that I just remembered. Thank Luisa for the wonderful dinner."

Virgillia's memory of the pleasant hours spent with Donald, Bettina, Ronerto, and Luisa vanished when Tommy knocked her roomy oxfords against the kitchen door and said, "Virgillia. Donald said he forgot a nine o'clock appointment that he must keep tonight. Luisa, he thanks you for the good dinner. He won't return."

Virgillia spent a sleepless night. Why didn't Donald return to tell her of his forgotten appointment. She would have been disappointed but would not be perplexed as she now felt. How trusting she had been, believing Donald had enjoyed her family and the dinner that Luisa and she took such pains to prepare. She was anxious to get back to the office on Monday morning.

The round-faced beaming maid met Donald on his return home.

"Well?" she asked Donald anxiously, noting Donald's downcast face. Earlier in the day when she had asked him if he wanted steak for dinner he told her that he was having dinner with a beautiful girl, his secretary, at her home.

"Well?" mimicked Donald without smiling.

"Did you enjoy your dinner?" she asked with concern.

"Good night," he said curtly and closed the door of his room, leaving Amanda staring open-mouthed at his closed door.

Donald tried to relax between the cool folds of sweet smelling linens in the darkened room. He breathed deeply of the fresh gusts of wind blowing from the open window but he felt restless. He tried not to think of Virgillia. He had had such a pleasant day with the loveable children in Virgillia's decrepit parlor. The chicken with mushrooms was delicious. Roberto and Bettina had been pleasant company. He even liked the way Signora Derella hovered over the girls while their parents were away. Why had he taken Virgillia for granted. Over and over he thought of Tommy's words whispered in his ear.

He had been offered an assignment at his former office in Boston with a large increase in salary. The offer was still open. He would accept it on Monday. If only he could remove the weight of his disappointment from the pit of his stomach. He wanted to get away, far, far away from Virgillia, away from any woman who could hurt him.

SIXTEEN

Francesco, Maria, and Rosalia had arrived home with a crash and a bang. They had returned a few moments before Virgillia arrived from the office. Virgillia stood near the door unnoticed, listening to Rosalia's indignant barrage. Rosalia had been home long enough to notice the scorched paint on the closet, the sofa which the children had so nicely caved in, the chipped cups and saucers which Luisa mentally saw as knocked off the shelf, and the dresses which Luisa and Virgillia had cut and sewed with such care which Rosalia insisted were ill fitting. Francesco was irritated that Luigi and Salvatore had not visited Luisa as they had promised. He had felt sure that on his return he would have news of a suitor for Virgillia. The fault finding naturally found vent on Virgillia as soon as they laid eyes on her. Luisa, they claimed, living so far away from them, did not belong to their intimate family circle any longer. She was not familiar with their family routine and their problems. She, Virgillia, the oldest unmarried daughter had been left in charge and had failed miserably.

Virgillia felt too hurt about Donald's actions toward her to care what her father, mother, and Bettina thought or said about her. She had seen Donald for a fleeting moment when he entered the office. He had ignored her completely. After lunch, she heard that he would no longer be with the New York office. He was being transferred to the Boston office from where he came originally.

During the hot flow of words as Virgillia changed from her office dress into her housedress, she had time to notice many things. Francesco's small eyes shone brighter. He held his head a bit more arrogantly with even a trace of haughtiness, as he talked, scolded and commanded his regiment of daughters. Ma seemed a little worn. She had lost weight. Instead of complimenting her figure, it only made her body seem drained and her face droopy, but Maria's eyes were eloquently bright, betraying a contented satisfaction. Where was the infant? wondered Virgillia. Where were the hilarious neighbors laughingly praising the Vinas' unfaltering stock in girls. Tomasina must have read Virgillia's puzzled expression and, wishing to divert Francesco's thoughts from the various troubles in which she figured prominently, shouted above the scolding voices, "Virgie, ma had a baby brother for us but he died. Pa said the little boy didn't want to come because he would find it lonesome among so many girls."

"Poor little soul," thought Virgillia as she bent to kiss her mother. At any rate, she wouldn't have any diapers to wash. She caught the reflection of ma's victory in pa's eyes as they exchanged fleeting glances. Maria had given Francesco a son. They had a little angel in heaven praying for them, Maria said contentedly.

Giuseppe had called a taxi as soon as he knew that Rosalia, Maria, and Francesco were returning home. He settled Luisa, her children, and the luggage in the car. Giuseppe and Luisa both agreed that as long as there was no baby to welcome, there would be more room for the family, if she left before they arrived. Luisa had been glad to get away before pa, ma, and Rosalia returned. She knew all the faults Rosalia would find with their mismanagement of the household. Dutifully Luisa had cooked supper for the entire family. Virgillia now set the table and helped the children with their supper, while Maria relaxed in her favorite chair and happily looked over her children.

Virgillia knew that ma had missed each and every one of them. She had missed ma too. Ma didn't care how many cups were broken, how badly her best blanket was scorched, and how burnt the closet was as long as she had found her children as healthy as when she had left them, she said. That quieted Rosalia and pa. Ma's eyes then strayed to the Madonna. Her glance fell on the cow's horns nailed underneath the picture of the Madonna. Virgillia followed her glance. She then told her how Signora Derella had placed them there because she didn't believe any longer in their power. She wanted the Madonna to see that she wasn't using them. Maria was pleased. Even pa and Rosalia took time to smile. The Madonna through God would keep Bettina close to her side. She was giving Bettina a healthy minded mother-in-law. God be praised, thought Maria relieved.

That evening when they were half through with supper, Tommy grinned mischievously at Virgillia, then handed Rosalia a long, white envelope.

"Luisa left this for you Rosalia. She said you are to read it at suppertime when the family is together."

"Why didn't you give it to me before, Tommy," scolded Rosalia, thinking the letter must be a plea to excuse her from all the mishaps which had occurred while managing ma's family.

"Luisa said the news is very important and you should read it to ma and pa," said Tommy.

Dear ma, pa, and Rosalia,

I left before you came home to avoid confusion for ma's sake. She'll need rest. I'll visit some Sunday with the family. While you were away, I entertained Virgillia's boyfriend from the office. He is a very fine fellow. I think they are in love.

Don't have Luigi and Salvatore bring a suitor for Virgillia because love is where you find it, and Virgillia has found her love in the office.

151

I'm sorry about our little brother. God has chosen to give us an angel in heaven.

Love,
Luisa and family

Ma, pa, and Rosalia sat speechless, staring at Virgillia.

When pa found his voice, he said, "Rosalia, you are the only one I can trust with my family. Luisa had no right to entertain Virgillia's boyfriend while we were away."

"Virgillia, are you in love?" Maria asked sympathetically.

"Will you invite him for dinner on Sunday so the rest of the family may meet him?" Rosalia spoke with a touch of sarcasm. Her buck teeth glistened as they bit into her lower lip. She felt hurt. Virgillia had confided her love to Luisa and not to her.

"I would very much like to meet your lover," said Francesco helplessly.

Virgillia arose from her chair and clenched her fists, crying, "I don't want to talk about it. Do you hear? Do you hear? I don't ever want to talk about it!" She ran outside the kitchen and down to Rosalia's flat.

Francesco felt completely at a loss. He spread out his hands, hunched his shoulders, and rolled his eyes upward.

"Dear God, does Virgillia have a boy friend or doesn't she have a boyfriend?"

Signora Derella flitted into the room. She heard Francesco's words.

"Oh, Francesco." She opened her palms, folded them on her breasts and looked heavenward.

"What a wonderful boy Virgillia brought home when you were away. Francesco, he is magnificent!" Signora Derella tweaked an imaginary mustache. "Who is he? Where does he come from?"

For once Rosalia was short of words. What could she tell Signora Derella, what could anyone tell her now that Virgillia refused to speak of her lover.

152

"What are you going to do, Francesco? Are you still going to ask Luigi and Salvatore to bring Virgie a suitor?" Signora Derella asked curiously.

"We have asked Virgillia to bring her friend to dinner. If he doesn't come, then that means that Virgillia does not have a suitor. Am I right Signora Derella?" Francesco asked more for his own sense of direction than caring to take Signora Derella into his confidence.

"You are perfectly right, Francesco. Either she has a sweetheart or she hasn't. Roberto and Bettina can't wait forever. They want to get married right after Virgillia."

"Thank you Blessed Mother," Maria prayed silently as her eyes searched the Madonna's face. "Virgillia is in love."

Maria remained silent. She was grateful for many things. She was glad that Signora Derella was getting back to her normal state of mind and had accepted Bettina's evening work schedule with good grace. She had promised Maria to go to the five o'clock mass with her every Sunday morning and she was even anxious to go to confession and receive Holy Communion every first Friday of the month to prepare for her place in heaven. Signora Derella's problem had been solved. She had given Francesco a son. She knew that with faith Virgillia's problem would too be solved. Maria felt confident. Virgillia had fallen in love, but what happened? Why didn't she want to talk about it? Please, life, don't hurt my Virgillia too much, Maria's heart begged.

Virgillia couldn't wait to return to the office. She felt that Donald could not just fly out of her life like an inflated toy balloon. His private office was still intact. He probably had to leave on short notice and he would return.

When she arrived at the office, her heart did a somersault. Donald was in his office. She could see his shadow from the opaque glass window. Her heart tripped mercilessly. Quickly she brushed her hair, looked in her pocket mirror, picked up his mail and opened the door.

Donald seemed much thinner. He was friendly but impersonal.

"Where have you been?" Virgillia asked warmly.

"I've been transferred to the Boston office."

"Oh," said Virgillia. "Do you like it there?"

"I have no choice," he said shortly, without enthusiasm. He turned his attention to his mail. "Ben Worth will work here for a while," he said as an afterthought.

"Ma, pa, and Rosalia have returned home. If you should be in the city this Sunday, they would like to have you come for dinner," she said hopefully, much as a drowning person would pick at a straw.

He looked up then and stared at her for a full second, then looked away saying, "Thank them for me, Virgillia, but I will be in Boston on Sunday."

Virgillia walked back to her desk in a daze. Within the next few minutes she realized fully the futility of her dreams.

The receptionist walked into Virgillia's office with a tall, blonde young lady. She was dressed in black. She smiled at Virgillia as she followed the receptionist into Donald's office.

"How lucky you are to find Donald here today. He has been transferred to the Boston office," the receptionist was saying.

Through the open door Virgillia saw Margaret put her arms around Donald.

The receptionist on the way out smiled at Virgillia and said, "She was Mr. Long's former sweetheart. She went south to marry a childhood sweetheart, a doctor who recently died in a motor accident."

The receptionist went on her way leaving Virgillia alone in her desolation.

Ma, pa, and Rosalia had won. They had been willing to meet her romance all the way. They realized that she had really fallen in love. They wanted to meet Donald. She felt herself beaten. Had he suddenly lost interest in her when he learned that Meg's husband died? She saw Meg with Donald. Her eyes fell on the glass shuttered pagoda on her desk. With trembling hands she picked it up, looked at it for a long time, then went to Donald's desk and put it in his drawer. He no doubt had a date with Meg when he left her home in such haste, thought Virgillia miserably.

That evening she told the family that Donald had been transferred to Boston and could not come to dinner the following Sunday.

"If a man is in love, Virgillia, Boston is not too far away," said pa reasonably.

Virgillia fell into a fitful slumber that night, only to be awakened by the sounds of footsteps in the parlor. She felt a chill down her spine. The next moment she nudged Bettina.

"Bettina do you hear footsteps in the parlor?" Bettina who had been sleeping lightly worrying about Virgillia's love affair sat up in bed. The two of them listened. From the darkened parlor they heard a low murmur. The steps ceased for a few moments, then started again. Pa's voice was heard asking, "Who is it?" Virgillia and Bettina heard pa get up hurriedly. He lit the gas jet in his bedroom and slipped into Rosalia's kimono.

Virgillia and Bettina stood in the doorway of the parlor, their arms about each other.

"It feels like a cushion," said pa while lighting the gas jet in the parlor. In the dim light they saw Tommy kneeling on the middle of the floor, a white sheet was wrapped about her shoulders. An old lace curtain pinned to her hair trailed the length of the room. Francesco looked with consternation at boisterous Tommy, playing the bride in the middle of the night.

"Tommy, what is the matter with you?" asked Virgillia angrily. Bettina sat weakly on the sofa, staring at Tommy with wide open eyes.

"Tommy, have you gone crazy?" she asked with chattering teeth.

Tommy did not answer. Virgillia dashed the old curtain from her head.

Tommy arose furiously.

"Virgillia, you are always spoiling things. Give me that veil!"

"Why have you chosen the middle of the night to play bride?" asked Francesco, puzzled.

"Tommy, you frightened us to death," wailed Bettina.

"You're supposed to get frightened. Now the charm will work. Last year Signora Derella was telling the neighbors, while they were sitting downstairs on the stoop, that there was a girl she knew in Italy who wasn't easy to marry off, and her sister worked a charm on her and this is the charm, Virgillia."

"Poppycock," said Virgillia. A knock sounded on the parlor door. It was Signora Derella in her long nightgown and pointed nightcap.

"Don't you people sleep at night?" she asked irritably.

"Do you still believe in superstition, Signora Derella?" Francesco asked anxiously. Then he told her of what Tommy was doing and how she had scared them half out of their skins.

"It's a good thing Maria is a sound sleeper or she would have been frightened too." Concern filled Francesco's voice.

"Tommy, what you heard is a silly gossip of the old country. Let's work the charm the correct way. She took a huge rosary from around her neck and knelt on the floor. "We'll ask God through the Blessed Madonna to find Virgillia a husband, the right one for her."

The commotion awakened Maria. After Maria heard of how Tommy had awakened everyone with her superstitious charm, Maria agreed with Signora Derella to work the charm the correct way. Maria was always willing to pray a whole rosary. They all knelt. Tommy was the only one who balked, trying

156

to run back where Angie and Caterina were soundly asleep. Francesco brought her back by the ear. In the quiet of the night, their voices rose and fell as they prayed.

> Hail Mary full of grace,
> The Lord is with Thee,
> Blessed art Thou amongst women
> And Blessed is the fruit of Thy womb Jesus
>
> Holy Mary, Mother of God
> Pray for us sinners
> Now and at the hour of our death, amen.

"The Rosary is too long. We have to say the Hail Mary fifty times and I'm sleepy," whined Tommy, but she didn't move from her kneeling position, for Virgillia was kneeling on the end of her nightgown to make sure she wouldn't leave.

After every ten Hail Marys, they prayed the Lord's prayer.

> Our Father, Who art in heaven,
> Hallowed be Thy name, Thy kingdom come,
> Thy will be done on earth as it is in heaven.
> Give us this day our daily bread and
> Forgive us our trespasses as we
> Forgive those who trespass against us
> And lead us not into temptation but
> Deliver us from evil, amen.

Maria prayed, God lead not Virgillia into temptation, but deliver her from evil, amen.

Francesco bowed his head and prayed, "I give up, dear Father in heaven, in trying to marry Virgillia. Thy will be done on earth as it is in heaven."

SEVENTEEN

The following day the Vinas were marveling at the complete change in Signora Derella's thinking.

"Who would have thought Signora Derella would suggest praying the whole rosary in the middle of the night?" There was genuine admiration in Maria's voice for the miracle of grace wrought within Signora Derella.

"Only Signora Derella would think of making my knees hurt in the middle of the night," grumbed Tommy.

"You should have checked with Signora Derella to see if she still believed in her charm. She is unpredictable, Tommy. What she believed in last year she doesn't believe now," laughed Rosalia.

"Perhaps Virgillia is in love with this young man in the office and he isn't in love with her," Maria said wisely. The discussion of Virgillia's love life crept up at the oddest moments.

"Oh, let's see what Luigi and Salvatore bring her," said Tommy. Maria shook her head reprovingly at Tommy.

"This conversation does not concern you, Tommy," pa stated emphatically.

"But this conversation concerns me, pa," Bettina flushed. Bettina put her face in her hands and sobbed audibly.

Franceso shook his head helplessly from side to side.

"I saw Luigi and Salvator today," said Giuseppe. "They said that the Longobardos are coming to the Festa Della Madonna Della Civita social and they promised to bring their son."

Rosalie grinned happily.

The old four-story brick tenement in which the Vinas lived

had a huge cellar which had been divided into small compartments. Each tenant was allotted one compartment. Francesco had broken the wall between his and Giuseppe's compartment and made one large room. In this haven Francesco kept his treasured barrels of wine, part of his Italian heritage.

Although the wine-making season was months away, Francesco prepared for a daughter's wedding by washing the barrels and wine-making implements months before. He would drag the six huge barrels from the cellar to the yard. Washing them by carrying water from his fourth-story flat would have been an impossible feat. With Tommy's help, he improvised artificial irrigation. Francesco had found a long, rubber hose in the gutter, one morning, on his way to work. He had retraced his steps and carried it home. He now hooked the rubber hose on the faucet in the kitchen, dangling the length of it through the kitchen window, straight into the wine barrel. He opened the faucet and, much to his delight, the experiment worked. Tommy who was much attached to Francesco's powerful searchlight, suggested using it in the evening while the barrel washing was in progress.

On this particular evening while Francesco was shouting orders from his top-story window, Tommy manipulated the searchlight. She heard footsteps in the darkened hallway, leading to the yard. She turned the searchlight toward the door and flashed it on Virgillia's pale face.

"Look, Virgillia," she exulted with shining eyes, "pa is preparing for your wedding. He told us that you and Bettina may soon be married. Rosalie said you might have a double wedding. It will be cheaper that way." Tommy's square face grinned impishly, then she saw that Virgillia had disappeared Where could she have gone so quickly? She had not heard retreating footsteps. She flashed the searchlight up and down the corridor, then stood still. Virgillia had fallen in a heap on the floor. Her face was white and she lay so still. Tomasina ran back to the yard, flashing the searchlight back and forth, up toward their flat.

"Are you crazy, Tomasina?" shouted Rosalia as she stuck her head out of the window. "What are you doing with that searchlight!"

"Come down quickly, Rosalia. Virgillia fell on the floor in the hallway. She doesn't move. Come quickly." Rosalia caught the sob in Tommy's voice. She came clattering downstairs. Capably she flung Virgillia over her shoulder and tried to reach the Vina flat as fast as she could, with whimpering Tomasina behind.

With Francesco's help Virgillia was placed on Maria's brass bed. Francesco muttered helplessly to himself. Maria could only repeat the words, "Madonna mia," as she made the sign of the cross. She plodded toward the bedroom and felt Virgillia's forehead. Her mouth fell open.

"Rosalia, Virgillia is burning with fever." Virgillia was gently undressed and Maria made her comfortable under the covers on her big, brass bed.

The doctor was not alarmed at Virgillia's condition. "She has the grippe," he said. "Lots of it around." After the fever was gone, Virgillia remained pale and listless in bed. Maria asked the doctor for a tonic to give Virgillia more color to her cheeks. Francesco bought a quart of brandy and urged Virgillia to take a nip, as people did in Italy, when they were ill, to make the blood circulate. Bettina promised to wait even two years before marrying Roberto and would not rush Virgillia into marriage, if only Virgillia would recover. Caterina and Angie sat by the bed and sang all the nursery rhymes they learned in school to keep Virgillia happy. Tommy became her slave, ready to run any errand, as long as it would make Virgillia well. Rosalia kept her fingers crossed and prayed that Virgillia would be completely recovered for the Festa Della Madonna Della Civita social, which would take place on the following Sunday.

The office sent Virgillia flowers, with a note, telling her they missed her, to hurry and get well, but Virgillia felt listless and seemed disinterested in everything and everyone.

She had fallen in love with Donald and he had not returned her love. He had only been dating her, she thought miserably, to spend the time of day with her. Luisa had been right. She had said, "You'll become an emotional volcano and you know what happens when a volcano erupts." Now Virgillia knew. A volcano threw up its fire and then was spent, exhausted. That was how she felt.

Virgillia took the tonic, sipped the brandy, listened to the children's songs, thanked Bettina for wanting to wait two whole years before marrying Roberto, forgave Tommy for all her pranks, and promised Rosalia that she would be well enough to attend the Festa Della Madonna Della Civita social on July twenty-first. She even smiled wistfully as ma during the day would kneel before the Madonna in the kitchen and then before the crucifix at the foot of her bed, praying the rosary for her welfare, asking the Blessed Madonna and Her Son Jesus to beg God for mercy for Virgillia. Even Francesco, seeing the lost, vacant expression on Virgillia's face, told her that he would stop worrying about marrying her to anybody, for now he remembered there were spinsters in his family in Italy. Giuseppe, good Giuseppe had brought home a beach chair, which he had bought for her to rest in the sunshine on the roof, where she could watch the birds nesting in the huge clock on the steeple of the church around the corner. Giuseppe could not understand why Virgillia turned her back to the steeple. He did not know that the steeple reminded her of the steeples of Saint Patrick's Cathedral she had seen atop a Fifth Avenue bus with Donald at her side, long, long ago.

EIGHTEEN

The day of the Festa Della Madonna Della Civita social finally arrived and with it, a hectic fuss with the bustling Rosalia scolding, instructing the children as to their behavior when attending mass and at the dance. Her scolding, however, fell on deaf ears, as Virgillia helped the eager children scramble into their much admired new finery. Virgillia dressed herself mechanically.

She welcomed the peace which the interim of the mass allowed her before the celebration in the school hall. As she knelt in her pew, she thought of Donald. She wondered if he was with Meg now that she had returned a widow. She chided herself for being so trusting and building air castles around Donald, making him her lover. She looked for her missal in her handbag to follow the mass with Father Ignatius on the altar. She loved the sacrifice of the mass where Christ offered Himself for the love of all mankind, for the love of her. He died and suffered for our sins, she thought. Dear God, give me the grace to suffer silently as He did. Her eyes stung with tears, as she thought of the pagoda Donald had given her. She had been living in a world of unreality. Ma and pa were right. Just like Luisa and Rosalia had accepted their niches in life and were content she too would have to accept what life would offer her and not what she demanded. She prayed that she be released from her listlessness.

The droning voices of the people uttering their prayers lulled her aching head. Virgillia kneeled in a world of her own, unaware that the people were slowly filing out. Tommy pinched her arm. Rosalia was outside the church, shaking her gawky shoulders, her face slightly upturned, her buck teeth shining with importance. Virgillia had to admit that Rosalia looked well with her black, shining straw hat with the large, white flower that she had borrowed from Virgillia's Easter bonnet. The black and white percale dress that Rosalia had sewed in a hurry for herself was a bit baggy under the arms, but it looked well. She was in her element as she grasped the Vina brood one by one as they made their appearance at intervals among the groups of people coming out of the church.

Francesco and his friends were paying their respects to Father Ignatius. The good priest nodded to Virgillia as she propelled her mother to the lunchroom where she would reserve seats for the family. The Festa Della Madonna social always celebrated their feast with a high mass, then from the church the members would go to the lunchroom where dinner would be served. The lunchroom was noisy with laughter and children's voices. The dancing would be held in the school hall, which adjoined a small open court, separating the school from the convent. The celebration would continue until eight o'clock in the evening.

Virgillia left her mother seated in the lunchroom and went to the hushed, sun kissed court. The quiet serenity of the small garden, the sweet-faced nuns peeking through their curtained windows aided in soothing some of Virgillia's turbulence. She sat before the beautiful shrine of the Madonna that graced a corner of the garden and prayed. Virgillia took a deep breath of the air filled with the scent of roses which grew profusely around the Madonna, then arose and found herself looking straight into Donald's deep blue eyes.

"Donald!" exclaimed Virgillia, then passed a hand over her eyes. She caught his shoulders with her two hands. He was real. She couldn't believe her eyes.

"Donald, what are you doing here?"

Donald took Virgillia's two cold hands in his and led her to a seat.

"I came because mother told me you would be here."

"Who told your mother I would be here?" Nothing seemed to make sense. Virgillia had a fear this was all a dream. Was it a dream?

"Luigi and Salvatore told mother, Mrs. Longobardo, that they wanted me to meet a girl, Virgillia Vina. They know my parents from Italy. They told them they know a beautiful girl by the name of Virgillia Vina who might want to marry me. When I heard your name, I didn't hesitate a moment." Donald looked tenderly on Virgillia, his eyes shining happily.

"Signora Longobardo is your mother?" Virgillia couldn't believe her ears. "But your name is Donald Long." She stared at him, not understanding.

"In college the boys found it easier to call me Donald Long," he explained, "and before you say the trite words life is stranger than fiction, Virgillia, I am the adopted son of Mr. and Mrs. Longobardo. They lost their infant when they came here from Italy at the turn of the century. They were heartbroken and adopted me. They have been wonderful parents, giving me a fine education. This is our secret, Virgillia. I am not Italian." Virgillia sat transfixed. She stared at Donald in utter amazement.

"I am an American. There is a bit of English, Scotch, French, and Indian in me, and when we have our children, they too will be Americans. Their background will not be one nationality, but many nationalities rolled into one—that is an American." Virgillia smiled but tears of happiness rolled down her cheeks as she buried her face on Donald's shoulder.

The school hall was crowded. When the Festa Della Madonna social gave a dance, law and order were thrown to the winds. Instead of a dance, the gathering became a friendly reunion of Italian immigrants with their American-born children. As the older people tried to dance, jostling each other at every turn, for the hall was crowded, the children would take the round, straw-backed chairs that lined the walls and would coast down the waxed floor screeching with laughter. Holding the chairs high, they would run several steps, leap on them then slide at top speed as the irate dancers hurriedly made room for them, scolding and laughing at the children at the same time.

Tommy was in her element at these functions. At this particular moment she forgot her plastered hair and high waisted dress with its puffed sleeves for which she almost burned herself and her sisters and yelled "wheeeeeeee" as she balanced herself on the chair. She flew across the school hall, not knowing where she was heading. The next moment she found herself smothered with Rosalia sitting on top of her and Maria, Francesco, and the Longobardos laughing hilariously. Rosalia pulled Tommy's ear and whispered.

"Go find Virgillia. The Longobardos said their son will soon be here."

"Virgie!" screeched Tommy, then her mouth fell open in astonishment for she saw Virgillia walking serenly arm in arm with Donald. Virgillia's face shone like a star, thought bewildered Tommy.

"Rosalia, ma, pa, Giuseppe, Donald is the boyfriend who came to dinner!" screeched Tommy.

"You little imp," smiled Virgillia good-naturally, now that she had Donald by her side. "You told Donald that I was expecting a husband any minute when he came to dinner and that I was going against pa's wishes."

"Virgillia, do you know my son?" asked Mrs. Longobardo, surprised and pleased at the same time.

"I am Donald's private secretary."

Maria, Francesco, Rosalia, and Giuseppe put their arms around each other's waist for support as they stared incredulously at Donald and Virgillia.

165

"Love is where you find it, Francesco, and no one knows that better than you, because you fell in love with Maria, at the fountain in Italy, where you both went daily to get jugs of water," reminded Mr. Longobardo, grinning pleasantly.

Now they surrounded Donald and Virgillia. They asked all sorts of questions, and when Francesco fully understood the part Tommy played in Virgillia's romance, he sternly called her.

"Tommy, come here at once!" but Maria tugged his arm.

"Franci, Tommy was working with us. Don't you see, Franci? Donald had time to see if he really was in love with Virgillia or if he still loved Meg, the widow of whom his mother was just telling me. Dear God, you are so good in Your Wisdom." Maria folded her hands piously and looked heavenward, wiping away a joyful tear.

Father Ignatius smiled upon his parishioners. Francesco and Rosalia tried to tell him of Virgillia's wonderful romance. The good Father blessed them all, and then Francesco, his happiness getting out of bounds, shouted, "Come everybody, let's dance the tarantella in honor of Virgillia and Donald. Happy romance, happy romance to the two lovers!" They grasped hands, the Longobardos, the Vinas, Signora Derella, Rosalia and Giuseppe. The circle grew wider and wider until all the men, women, and children, stimulated by the catchy tune of the music, hopped, skipped, and twirled merrily around and around the room. They pushed Virgillia and Donald in the center of the circle, giving them the floor space to dance by themselves, while the others danced around them, singing merrily.

The music ceased. Soda and cookies were passed around. Donald and Virgillia found their way to the quiet court again. Donald handed Virgillia a small package. She opened it, looked tenderly at the pagoda with the glass shutters. In the Chinaman's hand glistened an engagement ring with the largest diamond Virgillia had ever seen.

In the twilight of the court they did not see Maria and Francesco humbly kneeling before the Madonna.

"What a wonderful and strange land this is, giving freedom and equality to all. In Italy a Longobardo would never stoop to speak to a Vina. Blessed be God in His angels and His saints," prayed Maria as she fingered her rosary.

Their hearts filled with gratitude, Maria and Francesco now paid tribute to their Madonna. Softly they prayed,

Hail Holy Queen, Mother of Mercy, our life our sweetness and our hope. To Thee do we pray, poor banished children of Eve, to Thee do we send up our sighs, mourning and weeping in this valley of tears. Turn then, most gracious advocate, Thine eyes of mercy towards us; and after this our exile, show unto us the Blessed Fruit of Thy Womb Jesus. O Clement, O loving, O Sweet Virgin Mary, pray for us, O Holy Mother of God, that we may be worthy of the promises of Christ.

Back in the school hall Virgillia danced with Donald. Suddenly Donald chuckled. Virgillia looked at him questioningly.

"Tommy told me the truth, Virgillia. She said you were expecting your husband, and I was the husband Luigi and Salvatore were trying to locate all the time."

Virgillia rested her head on his shoulder.

"What is to be is written, ma says. I was fighting pa and Rosalia, while they were trying hard to help me. Now I believe in fate," whispered Virgillia, as she tenderly kissed him.